Loving Lakyn

CHARLOTTE REAGAN

Copyright © 2021 Charlotte Reagan

All rights reserved.

Written for anyone who needs to know it's going to be okay.

Thanks, sis, for all the help ♥

CONTENTS

1	Jeremy L. James Jr.	1
2	Living was Hard with a capital H and all that shit.	10
3	"Are you flirting with me?"	18
4	"Like tackling boys, huh Scott?"	28
5	He was the King of Bad Ideas.	37
6	"We should form a support group."	47
7	"No cuts, no drinks."	54
8	"I have sixteen years worth of issues stacked up."	62
9	"You want to make a porn star joke, don't you?"	70
10	I had half the mind to throw a full-blown tantrum.	77
11	"No homo."	87
12	Happy pill.	94
13	"I need better coping mechanisms."	104
14	"Why is life so hard?"	112
15	"I can give you the exact inches if you're curious!"	120
16	Did you know there are gay penguins?	128
17	"You're going to be okay."	136
E	Living was definitely worth it.	143

Trigger Warnings

Suicidal Ideation
Self Deprecating Thoughts
Descriptions of an Attempted Suicide Scene *(after the fact)*
Mentions of Past Child Abuse
Underage Substance Abuse *(marijuana, alcohol, euphoric pills)*
Descriptions of Self Harm *(cutting)* and Blood
Mentions of a Deceased Parent
Brief uses of Homophobic Language
Bullying
Descriptions of Disassociation
Descriptions of Anxiety

Loving Lakyn is a story about hope. However, it is a rough ride. You can find a detailed list of triggers on my website, charlottereaganauthor.com

Read safely, my friends.

1
JEREMY L. JAMES JR.

Fuck everything.

Why was it so damn bright?

The room spun, white walls swirling into white tiles swirling into white sheets. Everything was washed in fluorescent lighting and disinfectant, making my head pound and my stomach flip.

Someone was yelling.

"Don't touch me!"

Why was there always yelling?

My hands felt useless as hell, heavy, a steady thrum of pain coming from my wrists under the motherfucking *white* bandages. I knew if I could claw them off I could get to the stitches underneath, could pull them apart, and my blood would be red. Red. To take care of all the stupid white.

"I can do whatever I goddamn want when you're talking about my kid, Benjamin!"

"Dad's home," I muttered to myself, weakly reaching for the cords attached to my chest, scraping at skin until they finally came off. My gaze snapped over to the IV in my arm, and I frowned as I went to work on it next. I'd seen people rip them out in movies before, but this was one situation I hadn't researched.

If I was any good at research though, I wouldn't be in a fucking hospital. I'd be in the ground.

"Your kid tried to kill himself, Jeremy!" I heard my uncle shout. He normally wasn't a shouter. *"I think it's about time someone did something about that!"*

I snorted as I finally got my fingers to curl around the stupid IV drip. I wondered if I could bust the vein when I pulled it out. Would it bleed? Could it kill me? Could I use the needle if it didn't?

"'Kill himself?' Ben, please. He's a teenager. They do this shit, they act out for Attention!"

The door was open, which was something I hadn't noticed before, but my uncle walked into the room and slammed it so hard that the walls shook. I abandoned my mission in favor of bringing my hands up to my temples, wincing at the pain pounding in my head.

"You can't keep him from me!"

"Watch me!" Uncle Ben snapped, and then there were other voices. Nurses, possibly officers. My father had never been a fan of closed doors, and I could hear him banging against the heavy wood.

My uncle turned around and froze. "You're awake."

I cracked a smile, though there was nothing to smile about. I was awake. I had failed. I hadn't even managed to kill myself correctly. That had to be a new low on the sliding scale.

"I'm alive," I corrected.

"Barely," he said.

For some reason I was laughing. It wasn't a sound I recognized, and, at first, I wasn't even sure it had come from me, but I was fucking laughing. It was broken and hollow and dry. And I couldn't stop. Not until I was crying, and that was worse, because that hurt. It pulled at my chest, tightened my stomach, made my throat feel raw — gut wrenching sobs that I couldn't stop any more than I could have stopped the laughter.

Uncle Ben climbed on the bed with me, strong arms wrapped around my shoulders, and even though it didn't feel good, I clutched at the back of his shirt, buried my face into his neck, and let him rock me like I was a child. I cried so damn hard I couldn't breathe.

"Why?" I managed to ask, hating myself for it, hating him for it, though he hadn't done anything. "*Why?!* I was supposed to be done. I gave up. *I gave up!*"

Uncle Ben held me until I didn't have any tears left. Until I couldn't keep it up, and my breath was coming out wet and ragged but there were no more waterworks. I felt weak and empty, and like an absolute failure.

"Because, you aren't done here." He pulled away from me, placed a hand on each of my shoulders, and made sure I looked him in the eye when he said, "Listen to me, Lakyn James. You. Are. Not. Done."

***

My hospital bracelet said Jeremy L. James Jr.

I hated it. Hated my stupid name, my stupid bracelet, and the stupid fact that I had people coming in and out of my stupidly irritating white room just to make sure I was still breathing.

Suicide watch meant someone came into my room every hour. They turned the lights on, woke me, and Uncle Ben who was in the chair, looked me over and asked if I needed anything.

Yeah, I needed something: some damn sleep.

By the end of the third night, I asked the nurse if the point was to keep me from trying to kill myself again. When she said it was, I told her they might want to look into another method, because even someone who wasn't suicidal probably would be after being woken every damn hour. She didn't think it was funny, neither did my uncle.

I lost track of things after that. I was there, but not fully present, not really interested. Disassociation wasn't anything new, and the time passed quicker that way. Uncle Ben asked once if I wanted to take a walk outside, get some fresh air. I didn't, but even though he had phrased it as a question, it turned out that it was more of an order.

Being outside made my eyes hurt almost as much as the fluorescent hospital lights. I could feel the oxygen entering my lungs, leaving a piercing icy pain in my nostrils. Uncle Ben wheeled me around the hospital gardens, making idle chit chat about how we would probably be having a hot summer. He talked about Juliet and how she looked more and more like her mother each day.

Those words hurt differently than the wounds on my wrist.

I had to talk to a shrink, which didn't go well. He wanted to know why I had done it. "Attempted" suicide. It was frustrating, because I hadn't really *attempted* to do anything. I failed. There was a difference.

I was put on an outpatient treatment plan, which was shared with my uncle and not with me. I was pretty sure there was a cop too, and definitely a CPS worker. She talked in kind, soothing tones and asked the questions I'd wished someone would have asked me when I was a child and all alone and scared. Instead, I was older, and tired, and finally I sat up and pulled my shirt off over my head, showing her the self-inflicted scars that lined not only my arms, but my chest, my stomach, my hips. That showed my pain and my struggle. That showed my need for it all to just go away.

She blinked at me. Like she expected something more. Anger? An outburst? A curse? I didn't have anything more to give her.

"Get him out of that house," my uncle said when they were in the hallway, in a low voice with the door almost closed. "*Please.*"

They released me two days later.

Uncle Ben took me home.

***

The first time I got dumped on my aunt and uncle's doorstep I was four years old. God knows where the people who were supposed to be parenting me went. I had a *101 Dalmatians* backpack stuffed with clothes, sporting one shoe, and a black eye that I promised came from running into the dining room table.

My Aunt Lily had let me inside with a bright smile and unshed tears. She'd bathed me, dressed me in one of Rick's old shirts for pajamas, then fed me a grilled cheese sandwich and fruit snacks. My parents didn't pick me up for an entire week, and it'd been the best week of my life.

When I was seven, my parents left me for two weeks. I got home to a locked door, found the spare key under the windowsill, climbed onto the kitchen counter and used the landline to call Uncle Ben. His daughter, Juliet, was only a few months older than me, and we got to ride to school together. I had hamburgers for dinner, and watched TV before bed. After my father finally came to get me, I 'fell off my bike' that afternoon.

When I was eleven, my parents left for the whole summer. Uncle Ben found me alone when he came to talk to my dad, surrounded by empty cups of ramen noodles and watching morning cartoons. He took me home with him.

Aunt Lily was really sick that year, and they'd turned the living room into a big bedroom for her. Juliet and I had played outside a lot, went to the pool, ran races; but my favorite thing had always been when the two of us would curl up with her brother and Aunt Lily and listen to him read stories. Had we known then that it was one of our last summers with her, we would have done it more.

My parents showed back up just before the school year. Uncle Ben had taken me to get a haircut, new clothes, and new supplies. My stuff had matched Juliet's, like we were twins. For the first time ever, I'd been excited about school.

I knew my father was there that morning when I heard the yelling. Aunt Lily had tried to keep me on the bed with her, but I'd been stronger, and I'd wanted to know what was going on. My father said something along the lines of *"You have enough on your plate, brother, you don't need to be dealing with my pathetic son"*. Uncle Ben had been so mad I'd honestly thought he would throw a punch, but then my mother caught sight of me. She grabbed me by the ear to drag me out. I always hated that.

After that, my parents gave me a strict talking to about who I was and wasn't allowed to bother just because they were gone for 'a few days'. I had to learn how to make it on my own at some point and I couldn't crawl around other people's feet and ask for scraps. Especially not Uncle Ben's after Aunt Lily died.

It hadn't been that hard to take care of myself. School had provided lunch and breakfast, sometimes leftovers stretched into dinner. The weekends had been rough, but I'd made it. I didn't mind when they left. In fact, I'd usually preferred it. They yelled when they were around, screamed and fought, blamed each other for random shit, blamed *me*. I 'fell down the stairs' a lot less when they weren't home.

They were gone the day Uncle Ben took me to get my stuff, which seemed strange in a way, almost anticlimactic.

The house I'd grown up in was a modest size for Bridgewood, and for all intents and purposes, it looked normal. It wasn't a crack house, nothing was cheap or falling apart, nothing was broken. There weren't any real signs of the hell I'd gone through behind closed doors. At least not at face value.

What anyone walking into my house would see was the 'Welcome Home' mat at the front door, the fresh flowers on the kitchen table that was always set for guests, the family photos on the walls.

But I knew where to look. I knew which paintings were covering holes in the walls. I knew which windows had been replaced. I knew that even though the cabinets were filled with prescription meds no one had any real need for them.

There was a CPS agent and a cop that came with us, both of whom stayed downstairs, just in case my parents decided to show up. Uncle Ben said he wanted to be prepared, and I couldn't blame him.

His son, Rick, came to help too, armed with boxes and a sniffle that we all ignored like stereotypical men. I was glad Juliet had gone to school, because even though I knew I would have to face her eventually, I wasn't ready yet.

I lead the way upstairs to my room with an odd heaviness in my chest. It wasn't that I would miss the place or that it had any good memories, but that I'd never expected to have to actually *leave* it. Everything felt new somehow, and the finality of it was different than it had been before.

I stopped short once I opened my door, like I didn't know exactly what would be in there — a few haphazardly taped up posters, a desk that was still covered in unfinished homework, more clothes on the floor than hanging in the open closet, an unused skateboard and a backpack dumped unceremoniously against the wall. My TV was still on *Adult Swim*, volume muted, and it hit me that my life had just *paused*. Just like that. The signs that I had been there were everywhere, but if I had gone out the way I'd wanted to...

How long would that room look exactly the way it did now? Constantly waiting for someone to come back to it? To finish that essay, do the laundry, or change the channel. Would it have been frozen in some kind of morbid limbo forever?

Then, reality kicked in like a bad horror movie. There was blood on my bed, smeared on the nightstand, splattered across the floor toward the doorway. There were dark, dry puddles on my navy sheets where I'd placed my hands before deciding to sleep one last time, already lightheaded, barely able to move.

I was sure there was some appropriate emotional response I was supposed to have to a scene like that. Shock? Regret? Guilt? Shame? Sorrow? Who would have walked in on it? One of my parents, if my plan had worked right. How would they have felt? Had they seen it yet? Did they care? Did *I*?

No, I didn't think I did. I was numb. Scarily, depressingly, numb.

"Jesus Christ," I heard Rick mutter from behind me, before he dropped the boxes he was carrying and pushed by to get into the room. There was a trash bag in his hands, and he pulled the ruined sheets from my bed and shoved them in, but it didn't matter. The mattress was white. That was almost worse.

So much blood.

"We don't have to do this," Uncle Ben said, his hand dropping onto my shoulder and giving it a squeeze. "I told you we could buy you new things."

"No. I need to." I needed to end this part of my life, to be the one to close the door on it. To walk away from what had or hadn't happened in that room. I didn't need it to exist as a shrine. I needed it to be empty.

It took all day, because I'd never really cleaned before. There was very little I ended up keeping, mostly my school things and my video games, but I didn't want anything else. Not the furniture, not most of my clothes, not anything with memories. I had another chance at life I'd never really asked for, and if they were going to make me take it, then I was going to start with leaving this hellhole behind.

Uncle Ben left to drop off the boxes of stuff we could donate, and Rick and I were alone.

It was uncomfortably quiet until I heard the familiar roll of metal on metal.

My head shot up, but it was too late to do anything. Rick's thumbs were already

undoing the locks on my vintage *Spider-Man* lunch box, his brow drawn as he pulled out bandages, wraps, and Neosporin. I watched comprehension ease onto his face when he reached the bottom and heard him inhale sharply before he dropped the box onto the desk. The razor blades rattled. I wasn't sure how many were in there. A dozen, maybe? I held my hand out for it silently, but Rick shook his head.

"Come on, man," I tried.

For the first time in days, I saw an emotion flash across someone's face that wasn't concern, or sadness, or something that just looked *lost*. This was anger.

Rick swiped the lunch box up like I might have made a dive for it and glared. "Don't even try with me, Lakyn! You think I'm just going to hand you this shit? Give you the thing that put you in the hospital to begin with?"

Fear was a new feeling for me since I hadn't died. My fingers shook but I refused to give in. "Come on, Rick. I won't do it again, alright? I just — I need those. I need them."

"Why?" he snapped. "So you can rip up the rest of your body? As if you don't have enough scars?"

My hands curled into fists and the gentle tugging of stitches brought me back down to earth. I glared at my cousin. All of this was his fault. "What the fuck were you doing here?"

"What?" Rick asked, not following my abrupt thought pattern.

"That night," I demanded. "What the fuck were you doing here? I had it all planned out, no one was supposed to be here."

There was a beat of silence while Rick stared at me before answering, "Juliet was worried about you."

Juliet. I froze, processing, trying to remember the last thing I'd said to her, the last phone call, the last text. "I... all I did was tell her I loved her?"

"Lakyn," Rick sighed, and his shoulders dropped, like the weight of the world was rolling off of him. "We see you, okay? We're not idiots, we're not blind. Dad's been trying to get you out of this fucked-up situation since you were *eight*. Juliet had been freaking out about you all week, kept saying you seemed out of it, that she was afraid you'd do something. So, when she called, I came over. Of fucking course I came over. With 911 already dialed."

I remembered making 'jokes', playing off my suicidal commentary with a belated laugh. I hadn't thought she had been paying that close attention.

"Besides," Rick continued. "You never really say 'I love you'."

I opened my mouth to argue, but I realized he was right. My parents had never said it, not to each other or to me. My aunt and uncle did, but I hadn't ever said it back. Not until the day we'd been told to tell Aunt Lily goodbye. She'd said, *"I love you, Lakyn. Do you love me too?"* I'd managed a, *"Yes, Auntie. I love you."*

My knees gave out and I fell to the floor, leaning back against my bed.

I didn't remember that night, not really, just hearing my name. Over and over. My body moved like a ragdoll as Rick picked me up. Blurry vision and a spinning room before I'd finally lost consciousness. Before I'd thought *this is it*.

"I'm sorry," I muttered. "That you had to... I'm just sorry."

"Yeah, well," Rick said as he put the box back on the desk before he dropped down next to me. He sighed and rested his arms on his raised knees. "Don' fucking make me do it again."

"Okay."

We sat in silence, and although part of me still wanted to reach for the lunch box, I knew I could wait. I would have to, at least until no one was watching me.

"You don't own a computer, do you?" Rick asked, and I noticed he was looking at the empty spot in the middle of my desk. I'd never been 'good enough' to deserve a computer.

"No?"

He laughed and tilted his head toward me, grinning wildly. "Where the hell is your porn?"

My conditioned innocent response failed miserably under his gaze and Rick arched his eyebrows until I cracked up laughing. It only took a moment before he was too, and we were both grabbing our sides over it.

It wasn't okay, it was so far from being okay, but maybe it was the start of something.

***

My uncle had a big house so I got my own room, which surprised me since I was still on suicide watch. My own space seemed like a leap of faith, and one I wasn't quite sure I deserved.

"So, no closed doors," Uncle Ben stated, and I shrugged because that much I'd figured. He continued with, "It won't last forever, I promise, you just have to…"

"Not try to off myself again, got it," I muttered, and watched my uncle try to recover from the bluntness. I winced, sighed, and backtracked. "I'm sorry. I'm still not — my system hasn't really rebooted yet."

He nodded and put down the box he was carrying, stepping back to look the room over as a whole. It was already furnished with a bed, a dresser, and a television. Done up in guest appeal, but it was more than enough. The walls were white though, which I hated, but most of my posters hadn't survived coming off the walls at Shitsville. I'd have to fucking live with it for a while.

"Rick's going to be staying in his old room across the hall in case you need something in the middle of the night."

"Oh, dude," I groaned, "Don't make him —"

"I didn't," Uncle Ben interrupted. "He volunteered."

Great, I thought bitterly, pull the guilt card. Make me feel fucking bad about it.

"At least don't make him wake up every fucking hour," I said.

"Language, Lakyn," he tried, but it was half-hearted, and there was a small smile on his face. "Juliet should be here soon. I'm going to go make dinner."

I stared at a spot on the wall while I took a deep breath and tried to steady my nerves. It would be my first time seeing her since the 'incident', and even though I'd known it was coming, it still felt like a lot. "Okay," I said, then looked at him. "Wait, can you cook now? When did that happen?"

There was a pause. "Maybe I'll just go get some Chinese."

"Good idea," I said, something like a smile tugging at my lips. Then, without warning, there was Juliet, her backpack already discarded somewhere and a tentative look on her face.

Uncle Ben looked between the two of us, then nodded slightly and kissed her forehead on the way out of the room. She looked older than the last time I'd seen her, somehow. All tight jeans and a low-cut shirt, her long hair straight and falling down her back, seeming like she was the legal age to drink instead of barely legal to drive.

She had the same teary look everyone did these days, and she blinked furiously before she pointedly glanced away from me. "I'm mad at you."

"That's fair," I whispered.

"Is it though?" she asked, and we both ignored the hitch in her voice because we both knew we wouldn't be able to deal with it. "Can I really be mad at someone who... who... I'm *mad* at you. But I also love you and I'm so, so glad you're here right now. So, we're just going to move on, okay?"

I nodded, quicker than I meant to. "Yeah. Alright. We can do that."

Juliet ran a hand smoothly through her hair before she reached into her back pocket and pulled out a silver cigarette case. When she opened it and offered me one, though, I could tell the difference between cigarettes and joints. "Wanna smoke?"

"Fuck yes," I replied, and happily took one before she led the way out to the backyard and into the shed that had once been Aunt Lily's studio. Everything was mostly packed up now, since she'd gotten too sick to work, but it was still a comfortable place to hang out in.

Juliet settled down into a seat by one of the windows, picked a lighter off the sill and handed it to me. We lit up together and I took the longest drag of my life, dropping my head back against the wall, feeling the warmth of surprisingly decent weed fill my mouth.

"You need some posters," Juliet decided, blowing smoke out in my direction.

"I know," I said. "I really fucking hate white."

2
LIVING WAS HARD WITH A CAPITAL H AND ALL THAT SHIT.

I didn't know what the difference between a counselor, a therapist, or a psychologist was. The last one sounded fancier but I had a feeling the only real distinction was an extra degree or two. What I *did* know was that I had to see one.

It was part of my treatment plan, which meant I had to 'deal with my problems' in a 'healthy way'. It was fucking bullshit and I hated the lot of mental health professionals. They were all the same with their stupid searching eyes and their patronizing smiles. Promising me they would be able to help and talking to me like I was a child. Where were they when I actually was a child? I could have fucking used them then.

I wasn't naive enough to think I was the most mature teenager on the planet, but I also knew I wasn't average. I had been through more shit in my short life than most people even considered real. That alone earned me the right to not be looked down on.

I wasn't a talker, I never had been, and every session each new therapist started with a load of questions. I always left tired, annoyed, and irritated. The fifth one, Mr. Edwards, was probably the worst. He yelled, which certainly wasn't going to fly, and then pulled the 'I can't help you if you want to be the victim' spiel. I wanted out so bad I managed to rip a stitch on purpose.

That earned me a trip to the ER and a reminder that if I was willing to go to such lengths to hurt myself, I wasn't getting better, and 'outpatient' could very easily become 'inpatient'. The reality of that was daunting, and something I couldn't shake, even after my uncle took me for ice cream.

"I know you hate it," he said as he carefully spooned the brownies out of his bowl to pass to me. "But you have to try. Or they won't let you stay with us, alright?"

When I didn't have anything to say to that, Uncle Ben sighed. "We'll keep looking until you find someone you can at least tolerate. But don't you dare hurt yourself like that again, Lakyn James. If you're uncomfortable, or something isn't working, you either tell your therapist or you get out of there and tell me. If it isn't a good fit, it isn't a good fit, and we'll leave. Do you understand?"

Slowly, I nodded.

"Alright," he said. "Now, what do you say to a shopping trip?"

"Can Juliet come?" I mumbled.

"Of course."

We picked her up once she got out of class, and even though she fought me for the passenger seat, we both ended up in the back. Her gaze warily fell on my freshly bandaged right wrist, but I shook my head and managed to coax her into a car game.

Shopping with her had always been fun, and for the first time in a long time I felt young, weightless, and normal. I ignored the stares my arms brought on, laughed freely, and let my uncle spend too much money on what was mostly posters and hoodies.

After that, somehow, therapy was easier. It was like without the scars visible I wasn't immediately labeled 'depressed' or a 'self-harmer' when I walked into someone's room. I was sure they knew, sure that it was written down somewhere, but it wasn't splattered across my skin anymore.

I felt like I was being looked at as a person instead of a ticking time bomb.

By the time I got the stitches out, I'd managed to settle with a therapist. Dr. Frank Winterfeld was old enough to be my grandfather, and while I didn't particularly find him helpful, he was patient with me, which felt like something I needed. He asked me if there was anything I wanted to talk about, and when I said no, we simply sat.

Eventually I brought up the fact that I missed my school work. Not so much school itself, but I had always liked learning, and I had a lot of free time. There were still two months left in the year, and thanks to my little 'stunt' I was behind.

So, we discussed that.

In the end, Frank decided that I probably wasn't ready to be back in a school setting, but that I was okay to do the work if Bridgewood Academy would let me. Uncle Ben talked to them, and it was agreed that as long as my grades stayed up and I passed my finals, I would be able to stay on track. That was nice since I didn't care to repeat another year. Independent study came with a school appointed tutor that I didn't really need, but she was nice and gave Rick some relief when it came to babysitting me twenty-four-seven.

Juliet was still a teenager and Uncle Ben had to work to support all of his fucked-up kids, so, by default, Rick was in charge of me. I almost felt bad the day I watched him move back in, because he'd been in college long enough to have his own life, but then I remembered it was basically his fault. I certainly hadn't asked him to 'save' me. He'd made his bed.

I wasn't sleeping, but that wasn't a surprise. My bedroom door had to be open all night, which kept my anxiety levels right on the surface. I felt like a child that was afraid of the fucking boogeyman in their closet, only it had moved out and was taking up the whole damn house. Rationally, I knew where I was and that I was safe, but when I laid down that didn't seem to matter. Nights were the worst, and there was no way of dealing with them.

I ended up sleep deprived, running off caffeine alone and only satiated by the weed Juliet dished out when she got home in the afternoon. Thankfully, that at least calmed me down enough to get some rest, but I wasn't a fan of closing my eyes, even when she was the only one around. Cat naps kept me going, but I knew they wouldn't be enough forever.

I wasn't allowed to go anywhere alone. Not inside the house or outside of it. I could only stay in my room if someone was in there with me or if it was night. The only time I got privacy was in the bathroom, and Uncle Ben made it very clear that he was trusting me not to abuse that right. I was allowed four minutes to shower, and any extended stay led to a checkup. Rick didn't have to get up every hour, but he did stick his head into my room a few times at night. I was usually awake and would silently flip him off.

Overall, it was annoying as hell.

Uncle Ben was trying, I wasn't ignorant of that. He faltered every time he had to reinforce a suicide watch rule and looked like he wanted to give me a break when he dropped me off for therapy. He tried to act normal when we talked, asked about my day, the weather, how my favorite show was going — but things weren't normal. They were fucked-up. And I didn't want to talk about the normal stuff, because *I* didn't feel normal.

Juliet's company was the most soothing. If only because she didn't expect anything from me. She didn't need me to talk, or be okay, or do anything other than just *be*. She still got that look in her eye every now and then, but for the most part she didn't treat me like I was about to break.

Even though I was.

***

As the month rolled on sessions came and went, starting and ending basically the same. Frank's patience thinned, and slowly his frustrations manifested. He switched methods constantly, throwing everything he'd ever learned in some fancy book at me.

"Why don't you want to tell me things?" he'd asked once, low and defeated, almost a whisper. Like he couldn't grasp why I was so reluctant.

"The sky is blue," I'd said, "the grass is green. Those are things." Oh, *snark*. That was interesting.

He'd pressed his fingers to the bridge of his nose and sat quietly for a long time. It was almost as awkward as the first day with him had been. It wasn't that I'd thought he was mad at me, I wasn't that fragile, but I knew he was irritated. My being a smartass didn't help things.

I was right outside of his reach. He wasn't getting through and I wasn't helping him. I almost felt bad for him. He was spent, he didn't know what else to do with me. He'd tried, and he'd failed. It wasn't his fault, I just wasn't going to fucking talk.

He let me leave each session with a hand over his mouth and a tired look in his eye. I really didn't care how frustrated he got, I didn't want to verbalize my monsters.

I wanted to cut them out of my skin.

That wasn't an option though, so instead I did my best not to feed them. I focused on my school work, got lost in playing *Assassin's Creed*, and drowned in the pot Juliet kept around. I napped on the rare occasion and she offered me sleeping pills at some point, but I didn't take them. If they worked I wouldn't be able to wake myself up when my dreams turned on me, and that was almost as terrifying as never sleeping again.

I wasn't happy, but I was fucking trying.

That was the most I had to offer.

***

The first night I really slept was the worst. I woke up screaming and drenched in
sweat, tangled in my sheets so tightly I would have put money on the fact that someone was holding me down. Rick was across the room looking shell-shocked and I could see Juliet in the doorway.

"What happened?" I asked, heart pounding, eyes stinging with the threat of tears.

"Nightmare," Juliet murmured.

"Came up swinging when I tried to pull you out of it," Rick said.

"Yeah, sounds about right." I sighed as I leaned back against the wall, feeling sticky and gross and like I wanted to be absolutely anywhere else in the world. The other two lingered, clearly unsure what to do with themselves. "I'm fine now."

I wasn't always a violent waker, but it came with the turf of a violent life. I used to be able to wake myself up, maybe it was lucid dreaming or maybe I'd just get so scared I'd jerk hard enough, but somewhere along the way I'd lost that ability completely.

LOVING LAKYN

The nightmares stuck around. Any time I got too damn tired in the middle of the night and nodded off, my mind was a war zone of the house I'd grown up in. I couldn't pull out of it because my body physically wouldn't let me. It'd gone into power saving mode, shutting itself down. I was left alone with the feeling of my father's heavy hands and the image of my mother's sneer.

They were no secret of course. After the bruise I'd left on Rick the first night, it was impossible to hide what had happened. Rick tried to play it off but he'd seemed too worried to actually succeed. Uncle Ben, predictably, was concerned.

After about a week the waterworks started. I woke up at four in the morning sobbing, and thankfully, my uncle made it before his kids because I would literally commit murder if another person had to witness me crying. He'd asked what I needed, but the answer was a fucking lock on my door, which I couldn't have.

There were times in my life when I felt nothing, and times when I felt everything, and after that my emotions were hyperaware. I became panicky and anxious, which caused me to actually talk to Frank because I couldn't stop myself, but it definitely didn't make me feel any better.

I finally broke, and suddenly every small sharp object in the house became my best friend. Stray thumbtacks, safety pins, paperclips, whatever. If I could press it against my skin and let some of the crazy out, it was good enough.

I missed my razor blades, but I'd take what I could get my hands on.

***

Living was Hard with a capital H and all that shit.

The more time that passed, the looser the ropes on my freedom became. I still wasn't allowed to be in the house alone, but I could be in the shared areas by myself. Bathroom time got extended, and as long as the door was open and someone was upstairs, then I could stay in my room.

For the first few days, it was fantastic. I felt like I could finally exist without someone breathing down my neck at all times. But then the world slowed down. The farther from the suicide 'attempt' we got, the more Real Life continued. As a family we were moving on, and rationally I knew that was a good thing, but I'd never been a fan of life.

I was having a hard fucking time still.

I gritted my teeth and pressed my nails so hard into my palms I was surprised they didn't bleed, but I managed to talk to Frank a little. I spoke about the fact that I was both apathetic about the concept of living, and completely overwhelmed, with absolutely no idea how to handle either fact. It took me the full session to get it out, even though I'd only used a handful of sentences, and Frank seemed pleased that we were getting somewhere, but it made my stomach roll.

In the shower that night I'd skipped washing my body in favor of cutting through the skin on my hips, just to shed the regret. I'd felt better then, but also dirty, which was problematic.

The deeper into the month we got, the worse my emotional state was. It had nothing to do with my restless energy. Sex wasn't easily attainable when I had babysitters, cutting was a big no-no, and there were only so many drugs Juliet was willing to share with me. Apparently, I was making our habit become expensive, and I didn't have a valid reason to get my hands on enough cash to pay her back.

My mood wasn't obvious to only myself either, because Uncle Ben started taking Fridays off so he could attend one of my weekly sessions. It was awkward, which all of us felt, but somewhat productive, because having him there at least made me want to work harder. I hated letting him down.

Frank decided that although my current situation was far healthier than the last, it was also a lot of change very quickly. His theory was that it had been too much too fast, and that my mental state was fragile.

I'd immediately decided that was bullshit. I was fucked up, sure, but I wasn't *fragile*. My uncle didn't necessarily disagree, but he also thought the other man had a valid point. Frank decided I needed some of my old routine back, and together they discussed the options.

"Do not send me to fucking summer camp," I muttered under my breath, running a hand through my hair. Camp was an unofficial Bridgewood Academy tradition, starting from sixth grade through senior year. It was two weeks in the summer, and although anyone within the surrounding towns could go, it was often an elite crowd. My parents had started sending me mostly because it was a good way to get rid of me without red flags being raised, and also to assert their 'status', but I'd never liked it. I didn't like people, group activities, or sunlight. Summer Camp was miserable.

I knew I was fucked when Frank ended the session with 'now, there's an idea'.

***

Somehow, I managed to make it to May. Some days were good, some were bad, but the latter was definitely leading the race. I was struggling, but I was standing. The nightmares never went away, but I'd been dealing with them all my life, and once Uncle Ben decided it was okay for me to close my door at night, they weren't quite as violent. I still wasn't allowed a lock, but it was good enough for the time being.

My bathroom time stopped being monitored as well, and as long as I didn't disappear for terribly long periods of time I was mostly left alone. Getting to take a twenty minute shower after being so harshly limited was pretty much heaven. I didn't even consider jerking off, it was that good.

I took my finals at the end of the month, and it was surreal to walk back into Bridgewood Academy after everything. It felt too normal, and yet I was still out of place. No one except for the vice principal, nurse, and school counselor knew exactly why I had been gone. The teachers were aware of a hospitalization and that I had completed the year through home study, but apparently some rumor had flown around because I was avoided like I'd had the plague. That was alright though, I just wanted to get in and get out.

I made it through my tests with ease, spoke only to who I had to, then was on my way out. I'd stopped before I'd even really understood what had caught my attention, but then something like relief was flooding through my veins. A sharpener. Small, pink, fairly new looking. It was tiny, but I was *desperate*, and it was the only razor I'd come into contact with since I'd moved into my uncle's place.

I shoved it deep into my pocket and walked out.

***

Summer camp happened midway through June. Uncle Ben thought it would be a good idea for me to get some fresh air, clear my head, and do something 'fun'. The nightmares were manageable, and I hadn't had any recent breakdowns, so I didn't have a reason *not* to go. I tried my best to talk him out of it, but he wouldn't budge. Although, he claimed that if I had a legitimate reason I could call him anytime while I was there and he would bring me home. That gave me some leverage, at least.

He took me shopping before I left so that I could get some more appropriate summer clothes. I grabbed a couple of shorts and some thin, light-colored long sleeves. He didn't argue with me, besides the one comment to stay hydrated so I didn't die of heat exhaustion. We both knew what I was trying to cover up, so he didn't push me on the subject, and I found some comfort in that.

The day I left was an uninteresting one, which I supposed was a good thing. I packed up, hugged Juliet, then Rick drove me to the drop-off point. I asked if he'd be willing to run away with me instead, but he just told me the sunlight would do me some good. Sometimes he was too damn much like his father.

The bus was crowded with teenagers who had more joy in their life than I would ever know. They were loud and flirty and I hated all of them on principle.

Finding a seat by myself in the back was easy, then I pulled my hood up over my head, shoved my earphones in, and drowned them out.

From that point on it was four hours of staring into space and wishing I were anywhere else. There were three bathroom breaks and a meal stop, but I managed to keep to myself and glared at anyone who aimed a misplaced smile my way.

We made it to camp just as the sun was going down, and although Uncle Ben had decided to trust me enough not to sign Suicidal Brat beside my name, I still ended up in a cabin with one of the counselors. It happened to a few campers every year due to space issues, but it was usually upperclassmen who were planning on being counselors themselves. I wasn't surprised that my uncle had pulled some strings.

The counselor that met me introduced himself as Mason, he was a dark skinned senior and nice to look at. He invited me to the cookout that night, but I declined in favor of settling in. Which really meant I didn't want to deal with anyone's bullshit, but it wasn't like I actually had to say that.

He'd side-eyed me pretty hard over the ordeal before taking me by the elbow and leading me away from the other campers. Predictably, he admitted that he'd been instructed to keep tabs on me, but didn't exactly know why. Apparently, he'd been warned that I was antisocial, and needed a bit of a push.

The thing about Bridgewood Academy was that it was a small school, and everyone either knew everyone or at least knew of them. I was pretty popular in the latter category, if only because I'd come out the year before. There were few openly gay kids at BA, but I'd made a splash.

I didn't like lying, but I was good at telling half-truths. I'd had years of practice, between covering things up and redirecting people's attention. There were only so many 'accidents' one kid could have, after all. So, it wasn't difficult for me to manipulate my situation. I reminded Mason of the drama from the year before and stated my 'parents' were 'just worried' and that I was actually fine. Being outdoors really wasn't my thing, and all I wanted to do was go lie in my room for a while and play my Gameboy before the schedule made my presence mandatory.

Mason had seemed mildly skeptical, but also like he'd understood, so he checked me in and then handed me a key to the cabin. I gave him a mock salute before taking off across the camp. The counselors' cabins were at the back and smaller than the others, but it hardly mattered because they came with actual bedrooms. Bedrooms that had doors.

I threw my bags down before I closed said door, slid the lock into place, and rested my forehead against the cool wood. The silence was almost deafening, and yet I found it oddly comforting at the same time. No one was yelling, which was common at Shitsville. No one was whispering, which was common at my uncle's place. There wasn't the loud camp chatter from years before. It was just me. Me and a tiny razor blade in the bottom of my bag that could help me out if things got tough.

LOVING LAKYN

It was going to be a long two weeks, but it did have its upsides.

3
"ARE YOU FLIRTING WITH ME?"

Summer Camp was a fucking joke.

Somehow it seemed worse this year than any other time I'd been, although I really couldn't say why. The reasons ranged from the fact that I didn't have any friends to the fact that I was supposed to be six-foot underground. I wondered idly where my parents would have buried me. Probably in the backyard if they could have got away with it. Uncle Ben would have made sure it was somewhere nice though. Maybe near Aunt Lily, under the green grass and the bright sun and away from all the damn cheer.

I hated happy people.

They got under my skin.

Despite the fact that my cabin was mostly private, my schedule wasn't. I was forced to participate not only by the rules, but by Mason's watchful eye. He was like a less annoying version of Rick, because although he made sure I got where I needed to be, he wasn't invested enough to stick around. So, I was out and about, dealing with the obnoxious campers and the counselors that were constantly annoyed with me for refusing to smile.

I was in hell.

I'd died and been dragged straight to hell.

It was definitely hot enough to be hell.

The days were jam-packed with shit to do: horseback riding and team sports, crafts and workshops, and then of course, the lake. People tended to end up there during any free time or as the day was ending. Which was fine with me, because everyone wanted to be in the water. I was perfectly happy to chill on the sidelines.

The first day was a blur of obligatory introductions, the loudest breakfast possible as people got reacquainted, and then the lake. I claimed a picnic table under one of the few trees as my own, sat on top of it, and turned my full attention to my Gameboy. The water was probably more comfortable than the dry heat I was wrapped up in, but I had absolutely no desire to subject myself to that mess.

Besides, playing *Pokémon* was much more interesting. At least until I was rudely interrupted.

"Yo! Lakyn! Watch out!" My head snapped up and I dropped my game safely in my lap in favor of catching the football that was flying directly toward my face. I scowled in irritation and drew my gaze up to figure out where it'd come from.

Scott White. I hadn't seen him in a year, but I'd recognize him anywhere. He was taller now, still a bit lanky but with a nice new layer of muscle, broader shoulders and a sharper jawline. His brown eyes looked good in the sun, as did his wet hair that was pushed back from running his fingers through it. He was soaked, red swim shorts dripping, water trailing across his tan, toned body and leading to very interesting places. I wanted to hold him down and chase them with my tongue.

I was in trouble.

Matt Alvarez, who had always been Scott's best friend, came up next to him with a guilty expression. He obviously hadn't expected me to catch the ball. Scott glanced at him, shrugged, then held his hands up as if he actually thought I would throw the damn thing back. I didn't. I arched an eyebrow and sat it down on the table next to me. Fuck them.

Scott rolled his head back when he laughed and my stomach lurched at the thought of the things I could do to that throat. I was fucked. I'd always had a thing for Scott, I was just surprised it had stuck around this strongly.

He came jogging up like I knew he would, bright smile in place, and I leaned back on my palms while I waited. He didn't make a move for the ball, but instead stopped right in front of me. "Hey. Didn't think you'd be here this year."

"Yeah, me neither," I replied, and if my tone was as harsh as it felt with that double meaning, he either didn't notice or didn't care. He was looking me over, though the way his brows were drawn together meant he was weighing the temperature against the fact that I was wearing a rash guard. It was white, at least. I tilted my head toward the ball to catch his attention. "If I give this back do you promise not to aim at my fucking face again?"

Scott smiled more, even though he tried to fight it off. "Don't blame me, that was Matt's throw."

"Then I suggest catching."

"Glad to see you're still a little shit," he said with a laugh as he finally took the football off the table.

"Some things never change," I replied.

He grinned and shot a look over his shoulder before asking, "Do you play? Matt and I were thinking about getting a team together."

"No," I said, and watched his happy expression falter, which was interesting. I hadn't really talked to Scott since about sixth grade, and yet I still hated to be the one that made that smile disappear. I sighed as I picked my Gameboy back up and hit the save button. "I'll toss it around for a while, though."

"Awesome," Scott said, and I tried to ignore the way my heart skipped a beat when his grin was back to full force.

What a jerk.

***

The thing about Scott White was that he had a reputation. He'd been popular all his life, easy going, quick to laugh, friends with everyone. He was impossible to hate because he was genuinely a good person. He wasn't particularly book smart, but he was good with people which made up for that. He had fantastic sportsmanship, was talented on the field, and he was good-looking. He was the whole package.

He also had another reputation, kept within a small group of people. Secrets whispered at parties, names shared only with a trusted few. *Scott kissed boys*, after a few drinks, when the doors were closed and no one knew he was missing.

He was careful, but it wasn't like anyone would out a guy like him anyway. I hadn't known until the year before, but I hadn't been surprised. Scott and I weren't close when puberty hit and sex was everything, but his popularity had kept him in the gossip circles and, well, Scott White had never had a girlfriend, had he? It was a sad point to base someone's sexuality on, but then of course his name had started circulating through *my* crowd, and two plus two equaled gay.

He liked my presence, for whatever reason. It was almost jarring, because even though the camp rules said I had to be around for activities, nothing plainly stated I had to join in. So, I'd expected to continue doing things the way I had the first day: present, but disconnected. Scott was having none of that.

It was annoying for more than one reason. The first obviously being that I had no desire to be around anyone, the second being that Scott was fucking popular. Everyone wanted his attention, and no one was particularly happy that I was getting it. Which, fuck them, but also, what the hell?

Matt liked me, but he and Scott were the same when it came to being nice to everyone and everything. I'd seen the dude run into a chair once and apologize to it. His judgment wasn't to be trusted on a large scale.

Scott kept me close to him and seemed to take my apathy in strides. He didn't berate me for not caring if we won or lost a team sport, didn't glare if I fumbled over my own fingers when trying to do something, and shrugged off anyone else's complaints. He smiled often, laughed too much, and I wanted to honestly hate him. I wanted to hate him so much it hurt.

Scott attracted people like ice-cream trucks attracted children. He was fun to be around, I got that, but for whatever reason he made other people four times more annoying than they were on their own. They became idiots when Scott White smiled at them. I couldn't stand it.

I wouldn't get in the lake for that reason, no matter how much he asked, but by the fourth day of Scott's renewed interest in me, the decision was no longer mine to make. It wasn't necessarily on purpose, Scott had just been walking too close to me, Matt pushed him, then his desperate attempt to stay dry meant he'd grabbed onto me for stability. I hadn't been expecting it, and even though I was almost as tall as him I definitely wasn't as big, and his weight won out. We both went toppling in.

The cold water was an instant relief to my burning skin and I hadn't realized just how damn hot I'd been until I wasn't anymore. I came up gasping for air and Matt stuttered about a million times, trying to apologize. I shook my head and threw my hand up for him to help me out.

Like an idiot, he took it, and I immediately pulled the bastard in the water with us. Scott thought that was hilarious, and the full body laugh he gave didn't do things to me. Definitely not. Nope.

"Jerk!" Matt complained, and when he aimed a light smack to the back of my head I let him have it. "I was worried you couldn't swim or something! I thought I'd drowned you!"

"I can swim," I said, pushing my wet hair out of my face. "I like to swim, even. I just have a general distaste for people."

Scott threw an arm around my shoulders and I managed to only grumble a little as he dragged me close. "Well, you're in here now, you might as well have some fun."

"I have a distaste for fun, too," I added, and Scott ducked me under the water.

I actually didn't have a horrible time, but socially I was tired. I'd never had many friends, even before things got bad, but Scott had tons. No one particularly cared about me, but I was in their way to get to him, which meant occasionally someone included me in one thing or another.

It was going fine until some girl shot me a glare that was more hurt than it was anger, and that was when I started really paying attention to the situation. The fact that Scott stayed right next to me, talked to me more than anyone else, occasionally let his fingers trail across my hips under the water.

The fucker was flirting.

I knew he kissed boys, I just hadn't been aware he cared when he was sober.

Maybe my gaydar was broken.

Ha.

I tried to shove the thought out of my mind, but for some reason, it refused to budge.

***

If I didn't spend the day with Scott, I spent the evening with him. When everyone else was distracted he would slide away from his group of friends with a football under his arm and wait for me to catch his gaze.

I was doing alright at camp, for the most part. I wasn't sleeping well, but the private room helped with the nightmares, and my anxiety was generally low.

There was a freedom in being here, because no one knew what I had been through lately. People looked at me the same way they always had, and even though it wasn't necessarily in a *good way*, it wasn't the way my uncle and cousins looked either. Broken, sad, waiting for me to fall again. Here I was the same person that I'd always been.

Scott was an annoying complication.

I'd always enjoyed his company, when I was younger and even more so now, but I didn't know how to handle the attention he was giving me. I was used to boys who were out enough not to bother playing games. Straightforward transactions of 'you scratch my itch, I'll scratch yours'. Scott was tip-toeing, which made me wonder if he even knew what he was doing.

I still went with him every damn night, though. I couldn't stop myself.

I'd read once — on some stupid inspirational card — that five minutes of pleasure wasn't worth a lifetime of hell. Even though I'd thought it was one of the most ridiculous things I'd ever heard, it'd somehow stuck with me. I knew spending time with Scott couldn't go anywhere good, but I couldn't stop myself either. He was addictive.

He talked a lot, which I normally found annoying, but Scott didn't fill silence the way most people did, like they were trying to avoid awkward pauses or like they weren't sure what else to do. He talked because he wanted to. We tossed the football around and Scott rambled. About anything and everything. He was expressive, used his hands often, got excited over stupid things. It was almost endearing — or it would be, if I was allowing myself to find anything about Scott White endearing.

I wasn't.

So, I decided to call the bastard out. "Are you flirting with me?"

He stopped talking mid-sentence, his arm still raised to throw the ball my way. I watched emotions filter across his face as he tried to process what exactly I'd asked him: shock, mild offense, sheepishness. He was attempting to figure out how he wanted to react. It was an interesting process.

Finally, he grinned. "That depends entirely on if it's working or not."

A direct answer was surprising, but the fact that his smile was fake wasn't lost on me. He looked worried, but he was taking a chance. It was a brave, if misguided, move.

"It's not," I said, and held my hands up for the ball that he still hadn't thrown. "So cut it the fuck out."

Scott lowered his arm like he'd only just realized it was still up. His head tilted in curiosity as he regarded me, and I eventually sighed and tucked my fingers into the pockets of my shorts.

"Why not? I know..." He paused, licked his lips. "I know I'm your type."

I wondered if he meant 'has a dick' or 'made of ridiculously bright smiles' as my type, but I didn't allow myself time to ponder it. Instead, I moved right past it and answered the real question. "Because I know exactly what you want and I don't sleep with guys I actually care about. So. Ball?"

Scott's eyebrows rose and I sighed as I went back over my words, realizing this conversation wasn't going to be over anytime soon. I'd opened the door, of course, I just hadn't expected to be invited in. "Don't let that go to your head, dork. I meant we used to be friends."

"We're not friends now?" he asked, and the hurt in his tone was so genuine I wondered if he'd honestly forgotten what he had been trying to talk me into.

I was annoyed. "I don't do boyfriends, and I don't fuck my friends, so regardless. Stop. Flirting. With. Me."

"You don't have sex with guys you care about?" He repeated, like he hadn't heard it right or something.

"No," I said, and drew the word out as slowly as I could. Honestly, I'd known the boy wasn't a genius, but I hadn't expected this level of damage.

"That's completely backwards logic, you know that, right?"

I shrugged. "I never claimed to be normal."

Scott sighed and finally threw the football my way. I jerked my hands free in time to catch it.

"So, you're actually gay then?" I asked, because despite the fact that I'd been the one to call him out, I knew I only had a fifty/fifty chance of him admitting it.

"There are other sexualities besides straight and gay," Scott muttered, a blush rising up his neck that I could see, even with the distance between us.

"True," I allowed, "But I've heard you have a habit of fooling around at parties. With boys. Only boys."

Scott opened his mouth and I could feel a well-practiced argument on the tip of his tongue, but he took a good look at my face before he deflated some.

"True," he said. Somehow that one word sounded like it was weighted with both complete fear and relief.

He caught the ball when I tossed it to him, and then we were both silent. I expected this one to be awkward, but it wasn't, not really. I kept my attention on Scott though, watched his body language, the shift between what I assumed was panic over what he'd admitted out loud, and belief that maybe it would be okay.

I hoped it wasn't the first time he'd said it but I definitely wasn't going to tell anyone, so at least there was that.

"Hey," Scott said after a while. "Can I ask you something? As a 'friend.'"

Smartass.

"You can," I replied. "Doesn't mean I'll answer."

"Fair enough." He sent the ball back toward me. "I was just wondering where you disappeared to, at the end of the school year? I was talking to April earlier and she mentioned something about it."

I didn't know who April was, though that wasn't surprising. I'd never really put any effort into applying names to faces unless they interested me for some reason.

The subject change, however, was pretty awful. "Didn't know you kept tabs on me."

Scott shrugged. "People talk."

"Mm, I was in a car accident. You know my cousin Juliet? Terrible driver, she was behind the wheel and we hit a building." Juliet *was* a bad driver, and had already crashed my uncle's car once, so I didn't feel guilty about throwing her under the metaphorical bus. "Yeah, turned out that it was like a radioactive waste plant or something? Anyway, I got these super cool powers. I can show you later. Spent those last few months learning to control them."

Scott went from worried to annoyed in seconds, it was amazing how fast he could flip through emotions, actually. When he threw the ball at me it was too forceful and I stumbled when I caught it against my chest. Still, I could feel myself grinning.

"You are such a little shit."

"True, but you like it," I accused.

"True," he replied, sounding like it hurt him to say, before a small smile appeared on his face. "Are we playing a game?"

"I'm pretty sure all you know how to play are games," I said, throwing the football again.

"You're not making this 'no flirting' thing any easier," he shot back.

"I tried to kill myself."

Scott faltered, my admission so abrupt that it caught him off guard. The seriousness of my words wiped the smile off his face. "That's not funny."

"I wasn't aware it was supposed to be."

He stared at me like he expected me to take it back. I didn't.

A secret for a secret, a first time admitting something held close.

"Why?" he asked.

I shrugged. "Life is bullshit? It's all meaningless? Something about an empty void that sucks out your soul? The options are limitless, honestly. The answers are probably all true, on one level or another. Pick your favorite and run with it."

I missed the ball when he threw it again, mostly because he didn't put enough behind it to actually get it to me. I sighed, and wondered if it was worth the effort to take the few steps forward to pick it up.

"I remember when you used to do just about anything for a bit of fun," Scott said. "You seemed to like life back then."

"It was a good theory, when I was trying." I didn't like just standing across from him, so I went to pick up the ball and tossed it Scott's way.

"And yet, you still won't sleep with your friends." He said it like he was trying to pull some humor back into the conversation, but once again his smile was fake, and his joke fell flat.

"Sex ruins friendships," I explained. "In case you missed the memo, it's not like I have a lot of those, so I can't really afford to pull that crap."

"It's not like you try to be friendly, either."

I shrugged. "Yeah, well, less people I have to worry about hurting when I try again."

"You wouldn't." His tone was so confident that I almost believed him. "I know your family, you wouldn't do that to them."

I already had. "You know *half* my family," I pointed out, because although my parents had always been around to save face, Scott only really knew Rick and Juliet from school. "And not well."

"I know the half that's important," Scott corrected effortlessly. "And I know you. Or, at least, I did. You wouldn't do that to them. Not again."

"We'll see," I muttered. A lot had changed since junior high.

***

My mother had asked me once why I didn't talk more, which I had immediately known was a trap. The problem with her was that there was never a way to win. One day it was "shut the fuck up!" the next it was "are you retarded, is that why you never speak?". Her opinions shifted at the drop of a dime and I had to go with them, because, no matter what, Mother was always right.

I'd been talkative as a child but had learned quickly not to be. It'd gotten me in trouble at school, and even worse trouble at home. I had vivid memories of the way the insides of my cheeks felt when they split open against my teeth after a blow. At some point, it became ingrained in my mind: quiet was better. Safer.

My social skills were a joke, only even functional thanks to my aunt and uncle. Snark was instinctual, sarcasm a defense mechanism I'd picked up from Juliet, but overall people learned not to expect too much from me. I didn't have friends, I was too smart to be called out on in class, and the only times I got in trouble was when someone else was pushing me around.

Speaking wasn't mandatory.

Over the last week I'd talked to Scott more than I'd talked all year. Not just words on their own, but details. He hadn't even pried for information, I'd just handed it to him. He had that kind of charisma that made people want to spill their guts.

It was awful.

That morning I woke up feeling like I couldn't breathe. The regret of using so many words, of saying so much, made my stomach ache. The conversation from the night before circled through my mind on a fucked-up repeat, and I buried my face in my pillow.

I couldn't even put my finger on what I had said that was so awful, I just knew I felt like shit.

I didn't get to dwell on it before Mason was knocking on the door, reminding me that it was time for breakfast. I held my breath and tried to control the urge to vomit long enough to open my mouth and tell him I wasn't feeling well. He argued, but I promised him I would be out by lunch, and if I wasn't he could come back and check on me.

He left.

The silence was worse.

I had to get out of bed. I tried moving, tried counting in my head, tried breathing slowly. Nothing helped. My stomach hurt, my head hurt, and I was *tired*. Tired of feeling awful, tired of sinking deeper into despair, tired of feeling.

I didn't know how to turn it off, but I knew how to make it better.

I'd hidden my tiny razor in a pair of socks, but I knew exactly where to find it. I got it free, grabbed a bowl on the way to the bathroom, filled it with hot water and some alcohol from the first-aid kit, and dropped the blade in to sterilize it.

I was self destructive but I wasn't looking for a staph infection.

Then I jerked my shirt off, wrapped my hands around either edge of the sink, and pulled my gaze up to look at myself.

Everything sucked. Everything sucked and it was never going to get any better.

The scars were a reminder of that. They were mostly old now, faded, as thin as hair, white marks across pale skin. Hardly visible without the right lighting. Across my shoulders, my chest, my hips, my arms. The ones on my wrists were more noticeable. Thicker, longer, deeper — made with intent, not just need.

But they were healed.

I breathed deep, leaned forward and pressed my forehead against the cool glass. *They were healed.* As of right then, my skin was nothing but a collection of old memories. Past mistakes. This was the moment Uncle Ben had been trying to get me to. A second chance. Blank slate. Do over.

The razor sitting in that bowl was smaller than anything I'd ever used before, and it was a sign of desperation. A relapse. I flexed my fingers along the edges of the sink and slowed my breathing again. "You don't need it," I whispered. "You don't need it."

"And I know you. Or, at least, I did. You wouldn't do that to them. Not again."

I pulled away then, gently picked the blade up and dried it against a towel. I took a slow, steadying breath, pressed three fingers to the curve of my hip bone, and rested the sharp edge against my skin.

"You're wrong," I whispered, though whether I was talking to myself or Scott's voice inside my head, I wasn't sure. The point was I was weak. I wasn't okay. I wasn't selfless enough to consider that my wellbeing was important to other people.

All I cared about was the fact that my stomach hurt, and breathing was hard, and I wanted to die. All I wanted, all I had ever wanted, was just to die.

The marks on my hips were for regret, and I knew that was what I was feeling. Regret for talking, regret for letting Scott wrap me around his finger, regret for putting my uncle and my cousins in pain. More pain. Always pain.

I put pressure behind the blade, felt my skin give way to it, then dragged slowly, precisely, as far as I could reach.

The relief was immediate. I pulled my hand back so I could watch the red bubble up, and each drop that fell free took my problems with it. Each word I'd said to Scott. Each thought I'd had since waking up. I licked my lips, moved the razor down a few centimeters, and started again. The weight on my chest lifted, the nausea slowly disappeared. Blood traveled down my thigh in thin rivers, but I didn't care.

I was crying. The tears were hot against my face.

I wasn't okay.

"You're wrong," I muttered, moved the blade again, and started another cut.

4
"LIKE TACKLING BOYS, HUH SCOTT?"

Anxiety was a bitch.

I could feel my heart beating, it wasn't hard enough to be bothersome, but the acknowledgement of its presence was a real fucking downer.

My skin felt extra sensitive. I could feel myself sweating. Overall, I was extremely aware of my physical being and it was driving me up the damn wall.

It didn't help that it was as hot as balls. I was dying a slow, painful, sweltering death. Why did life hate me so much?

I leaned my head against the tree behind me and slid my fingertips under the sleeve of my shirt, pressing them to the ruined skin on my wrist and idly feeling for my pulse. It wasn't nearly as strong there as it felt in my chest. What a liar.

"Hey."

I glanced at Scott, who as looked fan-fucking-tastic in the sunlight. I hated him so much I could taste bile in the back of my throat. Or, perhaps, that was the lovely reminder of how much I hated *myself*. "I am not in the mood to deal with you right now."

"Asshole," Scott replied. I shrugged, unconcerned, and he continued with, "So, can I sit with you or not?"

"Not."

"Why?"

"Because this spot is reserved for people who can be quiet," I said.

Scott looked mildly offended. "I can be quiet!"

I snorted and glanced past him at where the other campers were happily participating in the sporting activity of the day. "Fuck off. Go play or something."

"It's basketball," he said, nose scrunching up. "Too much running for me."

"And football isn't all about running?"

"I don't know, basketball just feels pointless, I guess? For one thing, you can't even tackle anyone, so where's the fun in that?"

"Like tackling boys, huh Scott?"

He breathed out a shocked laugh. "You're insufferable."

"Big word," I praised, and pulled my legs up just in time to avoid getting kicked. I grinned at him, but the slight burn on my hips when I moved like that was a nice reminder of how much Scott could mess me up if I let him.

"I can be quiet," he said, holding his fingers in a Live Long and Prosper sign.

"Scout's honor."

"You were never a boy scout," I said.

"That's where that's from?" he asked, like I'd answered some lifelong question for him. He thought for a moment and then said, "Alright, Scott's honor then."

I shook my head. "I hate you so much right now."

He grinned at me. Adorable idiot.

"Sit down; but I swear to god you better not annoy me."

Scott saluted and dropped onto the ground next to me. The tree provided shade, but even with its help Scott was still sweating, beads of it sliding from his hairline down his neck. It shouldn't have been attractive, but it was.

He was awful.

Matt was playing the game, and despite Scott's supposed disinterest, he was watching everything closely, exhaling through his teeth when things didn't go the way he wanted them to. It was interesting, seeing him keep his comments back, because he'd always been a loud, talkative person.

His absence from the court was of course noted, which drew attention to me, which I wasn't a fan of. At least no one bothered to leave their post, but they did try to wave him over. Scott ignored a few, shook his head at others, and somehow made it clear he wasn't going to move.

I tried not to let his presence bother me, but I was too aware of him. Of the way his muscles rolled when he shifted position, how his hair stood up when he ran his hand through it, how his fingers curled in the cotton of his shirt when he got too hot and pulled it away from his skin.

I couldn't relax because he was next to me, radiating barely withheld energy and looking *so damn good*. The game made it midway between its second round before I finally snapped.

"Go away."

"What?" Scott asked, his head jerking up. "I'm being quiet!"

"Yeah, but you make my heart beat funny and it's disturbing my peace. So. Go. Away."

He somehow managed not to laugh at me as he dropped his arms on his raised knees and faced the game again. "That's because you like me."

"No, it's because you're a pain in my ass."

"I would be if you let me."

In the beat of silence that followed I watched the back of his neck go red and wondered if the girls who trailed behind him around all day knew what a *nerd* he was.

"That was awful," I said.

Scott laughed and I felt my stomach drop in a way that wasn't all that unpleasant at the sound of it. "It was," he admitted.

"Why are you still hanging out with me, anyway?" I gestured lazily to the group of people a few yards from us. "It's not like you don't have anything better to do than chill with the fucked-up kid on the sidelines."

"You're not fucked-up," Scott muttered, and at my scoff he laughed and glanced at me. "You're *not*. A little damaged, maybe, but I can handle a little damage. And anyway, I like you. You're refreshing."

"Refreshing?" I repeated, unimpressed. "Like ice water or some shit?"

Scott made a put-upon sounding noise and rested his head against his arms. "Why do I like you?"

"I have no fucking clue."

"You're being an asshole," Scott said, but there wasn't any real heat in his words, and there was still that stupid smile on his face. "Can I ask you something?"

"Same rules apply as last time," I grumbled.

He nodded and studied me before nervously licking his lips, suddenly serious. "I want to know why you did it. *Really*."

I hadn't particularly expected that, so I considered pulling a 'no' card and telling him to get the fuck away from me. I already had cut marks on my hips from talking to him, I didn't need more.

"I got tired," I said, and by the look on his face I knew it wasn't an answer that made sense to him, so I tried to find the right words. "It's like when you have a day that you just don't want to get out of bed, like you can't find the energy or the desire to start your day at all. Your body is heavy and your mind is fuzzy but you think 'alright, if I get up, I can go get my favorite coffee.' So, you manage to pull your clothes on and make it down the block to get some, but they're out. You leave, and it starts raining. So you're cold, and you're wet, and you didn't grab an umbrella. And when you finally make it home, you realize you locked yourself out. So you sit there on the front porch, coffee-less, soaked to the bone, thinking about how you didn't even want to get out of bed in the first place. You know that feeling?"

Scott thought about it, then slowly nodded. "Yeah, I think so. It's kind of a 'what was the point?' feeling, right?"

"Exactly," I said. "Now take that feeling, multiply it by about fifty, take out all the frustration and replace it with numb acceptance, and that's how I feel *every day*. That's what getting out of bed is like, every day. Every single time, I have to find a reason. Even when it's a good day, I still feel like I'm sitting out there in the rain, my back to a locked door. And I just think to myself that I wouldn't have to feel that way if I was dead. That kind of tired is bone deep, and suffocating, and I hate it. And I hope you never have to really understand it, because it's an awful way to be. And I got *tired* of it."

Scott stared at me, silent, processing, then slowly turned his attention back to the game. He didn't say anything else, didn't ask or pry for more answers. Looking at him reminded me of just how tired I really was, because even with things on his mind, even quiet and unmoving, Scott White was so full of life it was sickening.

I was a little jealous.

"Be quiet," I mumbled, even though neither of us had said anything for a while.

***

By the start of the second week I caught myself laughing. It felt alright though, to laugh and not be right on the edge of crazy. I made it very clear that I was laughing at Scott and not with him, but he honestly didn't seem to mind, if his bright-ass grin was anything to go by.

He was annoying, but entertaining. Sometimes. Usually.

"I'll stab you," I warned him when he reached over to mess with my popsicle stick house again. It was craft day, which I had tried not to get roped into, but it made Scott happy when I sat with him and Matt. And the theory was that if I kept my hands busy then I could at least keep them off of him, but at some point I had actually become invested in what I was building.

Scott's smile was guilty, but he was still reaching for the side of my house. I picked up a stick and turned to him. "Straight through your eye, Scott , I swear to god."

"Whatever," Scott said, "my eyes are too pretty for even you to hate."

"You're pathetic."

He smiled at me again but tore his attention away when Matt nudged him. A girl was walking up. She was cute, long dark hair pulled back and bright shorts, and her attention was zeroed in on Scott.

He settled back into his seat, closer to me than he had been before, and plastered on what I had begun to call his 'everyday smile'. It reminded me slightly of the way people had resting bitch faces, only on the opposite end of the spectrum. Easy, natural, and not personal in the least.

"Kaitlynn!"

Her own smile was definitely personal. She greeted him the same way as she leaned across the table, and I tried my hardest not to scowl while I pulled my sticks closer. I was not going to lose my house because of her flirting.

"What are you doing after this? I was going to go to the lake, wanted to know if you'd like to join me?" she asked hopefully.

Under the table, Scott's hand settled on my thigh, fingers curling toward the inseam of my shorts. I shot a quick glance at him, but didn't say anything.

People were around Scott all the time, the girls usually trying to get his attention, but I'd never taken the time to watch his reaction. Somehow, I'd just assumed, with the way he treated me, that he was flirty by nature.

He wasn't. He regarded Kaitlynn with complete politeness, but his body language made it clear he wasn't interested, and his gaze stayed on her face instead of the cleavage her tank was showing off with the way she was leaning.

"Actually, I already have plans. Going hiking later, you know."

I *did not* hike.

"Oh, well." Kaitlynn smiled again and shrugged nonchalantly. "I like hiking, maybe I could tag along? I've been dying to spend some time with you this week! I feel like I haven't seen you in forever."

She was trying, but too hard, and I couldn't decide if it was in a desperate kind of way or if there was something else going on.

"Actually, it's a guys only kind of thing," Scott explained gently, his touch sliding down the inside of my thigh some more. I was thankful for the distraction, because it kept me from mentioning that a lot of things in Scott's life were *'guys only'*.

I shifted in my seat and dropped my hand to grab his, which did absolutely no good, because he just hooked his pinkie over mine and held on. "I mean, maybe we can all get a group of friends together and go again sometime, but yeah, I'm not really at liberty to invite anyone to this thing."

Not like the hiking grounds weren't public domain or anything.

Kaitlynn's shoulders dropped, but her spirits stayed high as she nodded and pushed away from the table. "Okay, that's fine! Next time then?"

"Of course," he said, and waved with his free hand when she left.

"So," Matt drawled from beside him, not looking up from his own popsicle stick project. "Who are these guys you're going hiking with? Because I know I wasn't invited."

Sometimes, I wondered how much Matt knew.

Scott laughed breathlessly. "I'm not going hiking, she's just not really my type and I'm trying to let her down easy."

Still, his grip on my thigh tightened, and I knew exactly what that meant. He and I were going hiking, or at least getting away from the other campers. I saw Matt smirk down at the table, but Scott didn't, because he was shifting nervously. It happened from time to time, whenever he realized he was flirting with me and he was sober.

I knew I shouldn't, but I still twisted my hand around until our fingers slid together and gave him a squeeze. Five minutes of pleasure...

***

I went hiking with Scott after dinner, and it wasn't as horrible as I figured it would have been. He knew the trails from years before, and it'd been a while since I'd actually enjoyed physical activity. I'd been into track during middle school, but I'd dropped out when life got hard, and I found myself missing the slight burn in my muscles.

Scott was good company. He somehow still had things to talk about, even though I'd been with him for most of the last week, and he kept my pace as we walked, occasionally bumping his shoulder against mine.

It was fine, until he decided he could just *hold my hand*. Which, although I'd held his earlier, wasn't cool.

"Don't," I said when his fingers closed around mine.

"Why?" Scott whined, dropping his head but not letting me go.

"You're *flirting*." I stopped walking and Scott attempted to keep going, but there was no way I was giving in, so his choices were to either let me go or stop to hold on. He picked the latter.

His head tilted as he studied me, then he grinned like he'd figured something genius out. "I am not! I'm just holding onto you because I'm afraid I'll trip."

"You're a liar," I pointed out.

"You could get your hand back if you really wanted to."

"And I'm a masochist," I conceded. "What a pretty pair we make. Let me go."

He did, but I watched the cheer fall from his face as my arm dropped back to my side. His hand went to rub the back of his neck, then he sighed. "Why is it such an awful thing to like me?"

"Have I not explained this clearly enough for you? I don't do boyfriends, I don't do sex with friends, so what would be the point of liking you? It's not like you're out anyway, Scott. You don't want someone you can walk through the school halls with your arm around their shoulders. If you did, you would have gone with Kaitlynn tonight, not me."

He didn't have a reply to that, but he didn't move either. His gaze stayed firmly on the ground. Finally, he said, "Well, maybe I don't want to be just friends, but it's not like I've asked you to drop your pants and let me suck your dick yet, either. So can you stop listening to the things people say about me and start listening to me instead?"

It still didn't answer my question, but he did pose a good point. I was making judgements about Scott without actually bothering to listen to him.

"What is it you like about me so much, anyway?"

"Shut up," Scott muttered.

"I'm serious," I replied. We'd joked about this before, but I wasn't now. "Is it my undying apathy? My distaste for fun? My suicidal ideation?"

I could have gone on, but Scott interrupted me. "You're real," he said.

"What?"

Scott sighed and looked up. "You're real. No games, no pretenses, no fake smiles. Your cards are all on the table. You're actually funny and I enjoy being around you. You make my day better. I like that people like me, I like that I'm the guy who people want to be around all the time, but do you see them? Most of them aren't even half the person you are. They're pretending, in the hopes that I'll like them back. You're not."

"They're still figuring out who they are," I defended, although admittedly weakly.

Scott shrugged. "You already know who you are. I like that."

"You can't fix me."

"I'm not trying to."

There was a beat of silence before I finally sighed and gave up. It felt like defeat, but I didn't really mind losing. "Okay."

"Okay?" Scott asked.

I held out my hand, and tried my best to ignore the way my heart skipped when he smiled at me and twined his fingers through mine again.

"I don't like you," I told him.

"Liar," he answered with a wink.

Motherfucker.

***

Camp came to a close without anything terribly interesting happening. Scott kept most of my attention by either politely sidelining everyone else or dragging me into his horde of admirers. It was interesting to watch him navigate, and even more interesting to experience his refusal to let me draw into myself.

At some point, I stopped regretting how much time I spent with him or all the things I said to him, but the lack of that nauseous feeling when I woke up every morning was concerning in itself. I didn't want to get attached to Scott, because I knew too well that I wouldn't have him all the time.

I also stopped worrying about what Scott and I were to each other and just went with the flow. It definitely didn't stress me out as much, but I still tried to keep my own feelings in check. A childhood crush was quickly growing into something that could be possible, and I wasn't sure if I hated myself enough to reach for that and miss. So, I ignored it. I was generally pretty good at ignoring my problems. At least until they tried to swallow me whole.

I was actually almost sad the day that we all packed up to go home, and I managed a smile and a handshake for Mason who wished me luck with the new school year. I couldn't particularly use luck — a survival guide maybe; but I said 'thanks' anyway.

Then I signed out, tossed my bag with the others, and popped my headphones in as I climbed up the steps into the bus. I was headed toward my usual spot in the back when Scott caught my attention and nodded to the seat next to him with a slow smile.

Mr. Popular was smack dab in the middle of the bus, surrounded by people who were leaning over their seats or sitting up on their knees so they could talk to him. Matt was in the seat behind him, speaking quickly about something that was keeping everyone's focus. Except for Scott, who was still waiting for me to make a decision.

I thought about flipping him off on principle alone, but it turned out I really couldn't say no to the fucker. So, I shoved my hands in my pockets and made my way down the aisle with a nod. Scott grinned and jumped up once I got close enough, giving me the window.

"Sup, man?" Matt asked, and I shrugged before we bumped fists then fell down onto the seat. Scott slid in next to me and the discussion picked right back up where it left off. As usual, no one expected me to participate, which was great.

Scott spent most of the ride talking, sitting with his back to me, but after a while his right hand dropped down on my arm, fingers circling around my wrist.

My sleeves were long, but he was searching out skin, which would have been fine if the scars there weren't raised just enough to catch his attention.

His touch paused, but stayed, at least until the conversation died down and he could twist around to sit next to me. He pushed my sleeve up out of the way and I let him, tilting my head back to watch the expressions that went across his face. His fingers moved over the marred skin the way mine did time and time again, and I wondered if he realized that was what I was always doing.

There were other scars under the big one, more faded, not made like the ones that I had intended to end my life. Fits of self-loathing and a desire to die that hadn't been quite so serious yet. The "attempted" suicide scar stole the show though. Large, deep, freshly healed.

Scott looked up at me and I could see the question before he even had to ask it. I smiled sadly at him. "Suicidal," I whispered.

"Self-destructive," he whispered back, before his hand took mine. It was a brave move on his part, but our hands were also nestled between our thighs, where no one would be able to see, unless they actively tried to look.

Halfway home we stopped for a meal and Scott snagged a table for only us and Matt, and surprisingly, people left us alone. After that, everyone was mostly tired, and when we loaded back in, Scott and I ended up low in our seat, knees resting against the back of the one in front of us, sharing my headphones. Scott made a face at the music I listened to, but he put his hand back in mine and didn't complain.

"Let me have your number," he said when we got home that night, after having conveniently blocked my exit for at least fifteen minutes while he said goodbye to all his friends.

I heaved a sigh. "Why?"

He narrowed his eyes. Oh, he was finally starting to get annoyed. "I'll let you in on a little secret," he said, "when two people have a phone, they can type messages and send them to each other through space and time. It's a magical thing, really. Communication."

"Sarcasm looks good on you," I complimented as I held my hand out. Scott grinned in triumph as he gave me his phone, and I rolled my eyes before putting my number in it. "If you text me about stupid shit I'll block you."

"Mmhmm." He didn't seem convinced. I shot him a glare and returned his phone. Scott smiled and pocketed it. "So, I'll see you soon?"

I sighed but nodded.

He winked and got up to catch Matt. The two of them went off together and I shook my head as I watched him go.

Scott White was going to break my heart.

Or at least whatever was left of it.

5
HE WAS THE KING OF BAD IDEAS.

Because of my age, my custody arrangement had been temporary during the court proceedings, but while I was at camp, my parents had finally folded and signed away their rights to my uncle. It was an interesting change of pace compared to what we were used to with them, because normally they were stubborn and seemed to get off on controlling me. Juliet's guess was that it was because I was old enough that the court would not only let me testify, but would actually listen to what I had to say.

Even if I'd lost and been put back with my parents, I would have tarnished their name for good. It was probably easier for them to come up with some lies about my living situation. Either that my uncle needed the extra help, or that I'd rebelled to the point that they couldn't handle me anymore, or the likeliest option: they'd refused to raise a gay son. It was both close to the truth and would probably earn them brownie points with their stuck-up piece-of-shit friends.

Win, win.

Uncle Ben and I decided to go through with a full adoption. I had only a few years left until I was eighteen, but the thought that my parents might have any legal right over me at any point was frightening. On paper that made my uncle my father, which was weird, but it wasn't like we had to talk about it.

Even though it wasn't over, going home that night was surreal, because it *was* home. Standing in the living room, I realized no one was going to take me away. No one was going to leave me alone. No one was going to beat the hell out of me.

For the first time in my life I was safe. It was a word I'd never been able to use before, and it felt heavy on my tongue.

It was too much for me to deal with all at once, and thankfully my uncle and Rick gave me some space. Juliet waited until neither of them were paying attention, then took my hand and dragged me to the studio to light

38

up. The pot helped my overly powerful emotions and I fell into a comfortable lull.

By the next day, I was ready to celebrate, and Uncle Ben and Rick took a day off so that we could all go to the arcade, spend too much money on games, and eat enough greasy pizza to regret it for the rest of our lives.

Dinner that night was a cookie cake bigger than my head and if I cried a little while I ate it, no one called me out on it.

If anyone asked me, I'd still claim summer camp was bullshit, but it had done some good. It'd separated me from my problems, and I'd managed to come back with a clearer head somehow. Which was how I noticed I wasn't the only one falling apart: Juliet was barely holding on.

I realized she was sneaking out more nights than she was staying in, and I had a feeling she had more drugs than just pot on her at any given time. I wasn't sure if she was doing anything else, because despite looking a bit too thin, she seemed healthy, but she had access at the very least. She was struggling with life almost as much as I was, but I certainly didn't know how to help her.

I continued seeing Frank, although I dropped down to once a week and didn't really feel like I was getting anything done. The CPS agent checked in with me one more time after the court ruling, did some looking around and asked if I was alright. When I said yes, she officially took me off their watch list.

By mid-July, Uncle Ben sat me down and said that I was allowed to be off Suicide Watch, which meant I got an actual lock on my door, and could go places by myself. I hadn't taken Driver's Ed yet with everything going on, so people were still generally with me if I left the house, but they didn't have to keep an eye on me constantly. I felt guilty about it, because I knew I was breaking the rules, but I wasn't going to look a gift horse in the mouth.

I spent a lot of time with Scott, who texted the same way he talked — often and usually not about anything important. I got used to waking up with something stupid waiting for me on my phone. The options ranged from whatever random-ass thought he'd had first thing in the morning to actual questions to memes that made him think of me. He never really cared if I answered him or not, he'd text me again anyway.

The closer to school we got, the busier he was, but every now and then he'd swing by the house to pick me up. Uncle Ben didn't mind if I left with him, likely just glad that I was making friends. As long as I told Rick where we were going, at least.

I didn't fully trust myself to keep my hands off of Scott. So, we did things out and about: saw movies, went bowling, hit up the old school arcade in South Gate, shopped, even went to the gym on occasion. I wasn't a fan of working out, but I liked to run, and the treadmills gave me not only the opportunity to do that, but also the perfect view to watch Scott lift.

I was shamelessly digging my own grave, but I couldn't stop.

Sometimes Matt or even Juliet joined us, or we were dragged into a group of Scott's friends that we'd stumble upon. With summer slowly disappearing, everyone was out doing things, and he was easily recognizable. It was probably that damn smile, shining like a beacon even from ten miles away. I both hated the people who stole his attention and felt grateful for them, because they brought me back down to Earth.

Scott wasn't mine. He wasn't something I wanted or needed. And spending so much time with him would only mean trouble.

***

"You're actually terrible."

Scott looked amused and aimed his water gun at my head again. I scowled, but let him get in a forehead shot before I disappeared under the pool water. Scott was a member of the fancy private pool in town, which meant it was usually empty, but especially on Sundays.

We were completely alone.

When I broke the water, I reached for the edge of the diving board he was straddling, pulling myself up as far as I could and opening my mouth expectantly. Scott switched guns to the larger green one, which was filled with a lemonade-vodka combination, and obediently gave me a drink. "You're getting better at that," he praised.

I hummed noncommittally before dropping back down and pushing my way into one of the pool tubes we'd brought. Because Scott was so fucking gay they looked like donuts, and I'd claimed the pink one as my own a while ago.

Working out was definitely shaping up my body. The improvements were small and hardly noticeable, but anytime they were, Scott made sure to praise me for it. Which was a nice little motivator.

He looked good, too. Tan, bright eyed, dripping wet. There was no ground in exposure therapy when it came to seeing Scott White half naked and wet. At least I was kind to him and wore rash guards.

The lack of skin probably drove him crazy.

Not that he didn't deserve it.

"Man, I'm not ready for summer to be over," Scott complained before aiming the green gun at his own mouth and getting a drink. "I love this."

"It's hot," I muttered, leaning my head back on the edge of the tube I was in, closing my eyes against the bright sun.

"You're hot," Scott shot back.

I snorted and glared at him. "If you're going to break the rule, then at least break it for something good."

"You like my bad flirting," he said. "You think it's cute."

"I think it's stupid."

"You at least think I'm cute."

"I think you're an idiot," I said.

Scott grinned at me like he'd somehow won that argument and wiggled the gun in his hand. "Want another drink?"

I shrugged and opened my mouth.

"If I hit you in the eye it's going to sting like a motherfucker."

"Your aim is better than that."

"Do you really want to chance it?" he asked.

I sighed and slid out of the tube, swimming under the board so I could pull myself up again. Scott smirked and slowly cupped a hand under my jaw, using his thumb to coax my mouth open. I met his gaze while he filled my mouth, and swallowed thickly. It burned all the way down my throat, and I refused to think of it as erotic.

Even though it really fucking was.

I dropped back into the water to cool the hell down.

"What about you?" Scott asked when I resurfaced, picking up the other gun to shoot at the wall. He had a habit of doing that whenever he was about to ask me a personal question. He either looked right at me, or distracted himself. "Ready for school?"

I went back to my tube, folded my arms on the edge of it, and rested my chin on them while I watched him sloppily spell out his name. "No," I finally said. I wasn't a fan of lying, and Scott knew that if there was something I didn't want to answer, I simply wouldn't. "Yes. Maybe. I don't know."

He hesitated, then looked at me. "Is it weird? You know, because you thought you'd be…"

"Dead?" I finished. "Not really. I don't know. I've kind of just accepted it, I guess."

Scott nodded like that was a good answer, then grabbed the green gun and pushed himself off the board. He made a splash, and I glared at him when he came up and grabbed onto the other side of the tube. "It's a new building, at least."

"But mostly the same people," I said.

Scott shrugged. "New friends, though?"

"Don't bullshit me."

"What?"

"You are not going to hang out with me at school."

"Why wouldn't I?" Scott asked, offended, before lifting the green gun for another drink. He took a few, then offered me one.

"Because I'm gay, Scott. Capital letters, trademarked, gay; and everyone knows it. If you hang out with me all the time — well, you've said it yourself. People talk."

"People talk about me anyway," he said.

"Sure, a very select few, and only to each other. Come on, you're Scott freaking White, no one's going to out you. But if you make this public? People are going to talk until it happens by accident."

"It's not like people haven't already seen us hanging out."

"Summer and school are two completely different things." I took the water gun from him and stuck the end in my mouth, filling up.

Scott sighed and wrapped his ankle around mine under the water. "Why don't you ever believe me?"

"Because I know the world better than you do," I answered.

He frowned, but didn't argue, and we floated in silence. Finally, he asked, "Want to come over tonight? Watch a movie?"

My nose scrunched up. "Are your parents home?"

"No," he said, which should have been the reason I turned him down, but in all honesty, I didn't like his parents enough to be in his space when they were around. Still, that meant alone time, which I had a definite rule against.

Evidently this was something Scott could read on my face, because he said, "We can sit in the recliners and keep the lights on, if you want."

"Lights can be off if it can be a horror movie and you can keep your hands to yourself."

The corner of his mouth lifted into a smirk. "No flirting," he promised.

***

I fell off the metaphorical wagon only a couple of weeks later. Despite the fact that it should have been an easy day, I woke up on the wrong side of the bed. I hadn't slept well due to the nightmares, my mood was down, and every little thing was determined to go wrong.

I missed my alarm, couldn't find my dress shirt, tripped over my shoes, and Juliet ate the last of my favorite cereal. It was stupid shit to be upset over, and I was aware of that, but I couldn't help it.

I was anxious as hell and I couldn't get a fucking grip.

I was used to the courtroom, even used to the judge, and I knew exactly how this day was going to play out. That didn't stop me from feeling like I'd been punched in the stomach the moment I was introduced as Jeremy Laken James Jr.

It was my last court date, which meant all I had to do was smile, thank the judge, and I'd get to go home with a new birth certificate and an updated social security card. We were through the hard stuff, all we were doing was wrapping up.

I was sick and tired of carrying my father's name, so I removed it. I was legally just Lakyn James; spelled with a 'y' the way I'd started doing it years ago. There was a lot of comfort in that. Odd how a little thing meant so much.

I lost time. Rationally, I remembered being there, signing the papers, shaking the Judge's hand, hugging my uncle, leaving, going home, changing out of my clothes, and getting back into bed, saying I just hadn't slept well, but I was happy, not to worry.

Then everything blurred as I stared at the walls in my bedroom, hundreds of posters covered the awful white, but the dark colors blended together until everything was swirling, and I wondered if I was having a bad trip, even though I wasn't high.

My heartbeat felt too fast, but my body was sluggish, my head hurt and my stomach complained of hunger, though the last thing I wanted to do was eat.

Finally, I got out of bed and pulled a razor blade free of the tape that kept it pressed to the underside of my nightstand drawer.

A few times over the summer I'd gone to work with my uncle and Rick, because although they could afford to move Rick's schedule around enough to keep an eye on me, there were days when it was all hands on deck. I hadn't minded much, and had mostly spent my time watching the guys that were renovating the back office. It had been on one of those days that I'd realized they were using razors to scrape away at the old paint.

It'd been easy to swipe one out of the package. No one had even noticed. I took it home, cleaned it, and hid it without the intention of using it. I'd just wanted the comfort of knowing I had it if I needed it.

I stepped out of my pajama pants before sitting down in front of my door, leaning my weight against it and running my fingers over the thin white scars that decorated my thighs. I knew I shouldn't be feeling like this. It was a *good* day. But all I could think about was how fucking *easy* it'd been.

A few court dates, that was all. My uncle's willing signature on a couple of pieces of paper. I was saved. I was safe. I was alive and I almost hadn't been. I'd chosen my path because I hadn't believed there were any other options. Yet, here I was.

It was too fucking much and it overwhelmed me in a wave of numbness that I knew was dangerous. Even as I pressed the sharp edge of the razor to my skin and watched the red pool up, I couldn't feel it. I couldn't feel anything.

So, I cut until I could.

Thin line after thin line. I felt tears before I even realized it was because I was *hurting*. I let out a sigh of relief as my head fell back against the wood behind me.

Sometimes pain was better than nothing at all.

***

A week before school started, Scott threw a party. I hadn't intended to go, but I felt like I was suffocating at home. It wasn't anyone's fault, but school wasn't like camp, so my uncle was worried. I couldn't even fucking blame him — there were fresh cuts on my body and I still wasn't talking to my therapist.

Psychologist? Who knew. Regardless, eight hours alone in a building full of people who didn't give two shits about me was not exactly confidence-inspiring for the guardian of a suicidal brat.

Rick was back at work most of the time, which was good because it at least kept his attention off of me, but that left me alone with Juliet. Rationally, I knew she needed her father's attention, but I didn't know how to bring it up, especially while hiding my own secrets as much as I was. It would look like a desperate attempt to deflect and I did not need anyone in my business any more than they already had to be.

So, I avoided everyone and everything, and thankfully Scott provided me with a good way to do that. Even if that meant I had to sit in what he'd somehow managed to turn into a Hollywood frat house with a bunch of upperclassmen I didn't particularly know or like.

There was alcohol, though.

I was perched up on the bar in Scott's kitchen, cradling a bottle of Malibu, while Matt was next to me so he could use the window to smoke a joint.

Kaitlynn was there too, and some other girl that was hanging off her arm, both of them dangling solo cups of something that smelled awful.

And, of course, Scott. He disappeared every now and then to make rounds, because people would crowd him eventually if they didn't get a dose of his attention, but he always circled back and shoved himself into the space between my leg and Kaitlynn. The closeness probably wasn't good for her.

It definitely wasn't good for me.

"You're going to be in our building this year, right?" Matt asked, making a face as he took in another slow drag. "This is awful, by the way."

"Yeah, I'm finally in high school hell," I said, then leaned forward and plucked the joint from his fingers. He let it go with a shrug, and I grinned as I pulled smoke into my lungs. It wasn't the best.

"Wait, you're only a freshman?" the other girl asked, leaning over Kaitlynn to scrutinize me.

"I'm sixteen," I said. "I started kindergarten late at the public school and Bridgewood Academy made me repeat it when I moved over."

"You're going to be in most of our classes though, aren't you?" Scott asked. He was nice and buzzed, which meant he was somehow even more friendly than usual. It made me wonder how much he needed before he started shoving his hands down guys pants.

"Yeah. Advanced placement. Trying to make up for lost time. If I keep at it then I'll graduate with you guys, too. No one will know I was a repeater by college."

Kaitlynn smiled. "It's a good thing you've been hanging out with us then, you'll already have friends."

Matt was nodding along, but I wasn't sure if she was being serious or catty. Instinct says it was the latter, but I couldn't always trust myself with social cues. I still wasn't fond of the idea of going back to school myself. The previous year hadn't exactly gone well by any means, and I had a feeling this one wasn't going to be any different. I was too smart, too gay, and too easy of a target. Not to mention I was starting right back at the bottom of the totem pole.

Scott stole the joint and said, "I've heard Mr. Vera is a real hardass." I didn't ask for it back, I wasn't feeling great. Scott continued with, "I really hate Algebra, I'm gonna fucking fail."

"We can have study dates," Kaitlynn offered around the rim of her cup. "I mean, I'm no genius or anything, but I'm sure it would help."

I didn't want to hate Kaitlynn. She was a pretty cool girl, and if Scott was straight she would have probably been his type, but she was failing hard and no one was clueing her in on it. It was bothering me, and she was getting on my nerves.

"Yeah, maybe," Scott said, then nudged my knee with his elbow. "Hey, weren't you always really good at math?"

I nodded and rubbed at my chest. It was starting to hurt. I wondered if it was the smoke or if I'd drank too much. Scott said something else, and I watched Kaitlynn smile too brightly and put her hand on his arm while she replied.

"Oh my god," I muttered, took another swing of Malibu before passing the bottle off to Matt, and leaned down enough that I could catch her attention.

"Kaitlynn, honey, he's not interested, okay?"

"Oh damn," Matt said behind me, although it sounded like he was much farther away. I felt a bit bad as Kaitlynn's eyes widened. She looked between me and Scott before sputtering out, "I-I didn't mean-"

"I'm sorry," I said. I felt like shit. She tried to say something else, tried to explain that she hadn't meant to make anyone uncomfortable or anything, but it went in one ear and out the other as I slid off the counter. Scott caught my arm when I was tipsy on my feet, but I pushed at him until he let me go.

"I'm fine, I drank too much," I said as I headed for the doorway. The hall twisted and turned as I walked through it, a tunnel of colors and lights and bodies. Everyone was drinking, dancing, and kissing. The music was too harsh, and my head was spinning.

I shouldered my way into the bathroom and kicked the door shut behind me. It was quieter, but I couldn't *breathe*. I stumbled to the sink, dropping my hands on either side of it, then settled into a squat and let my head fall.

I shut my eyes against the world and tried to draw in some fucking oxygen, but it wasn't working. It was only when I saw my arms shaking that I realized I was having a fucking panic attack.

It had been awhile since I'd felt enough to panic.

There was a knocking sound that I wasn't completely sure was real until Scott said my name, probably not for the first time. I drew in a deep breath that stung and said, "Go away."

"Lakyn, come on."

"No."

I hadn't locked the door, but I still jumped when I felt Scott's fingers touch the base of my neck. "Lake," he said, "hey, what's going on?"

"Nothing!" I snapped, but my voice broke. I whispered a curse and squeezed my eyes tightly against the tears that I refused to let fall. Scott's hand wrapped around one of my wrists and jerked me from the sink, so I collapsed against the ground instead. It hurt, but everything hurt. I was one hundred percent in freak-out mode not knowing how to stop it.

"Lakyn, hey, hey!" Scott kneeled down in front of me. I glared, rested my head against the wall, and pressed the heel of my hand to my chest. My heart was going crazy. I had a razor somewhere… somewhere…

"Do you want to go home?" he asked.

"No!" I snapped. "I don't want to go anywhere, Scott! Not home. Not school. It's so *fucking weird* to be alive. I was done, do you get that? I'd given up, tapped out, no thanks, don't wanna advance to the next fucking level! Do you know how much life *sucks*?"

I laughed, I always laughed when I got upset, and it was hot suddenly, so hot I wanted to pull at my clothes, run away, something. "No, of course you don't, because you're fucking *perfect*. With your perfect house and your perfect family and your perfect smile. I hate you, I really hate you. Why do you like me anyway? Seriously. Do you need something a little broken to spice up your life? You should really get over that because you have no idea what a damn *mess* I am. You can't handle it."

Why was I still laughing? At some point I had made fists and I tried to unclench my hands, but I couldn't seem to make them work, and the waterworks were right there, right on the edge. Scott was trying to say something, had opened and closed his mouth at least three times, but I'd released the floodgates somehow. I couldn't seem to shut up. "I don't want to do this anymore! I'm so tired. So tired, so tired, fuck am I —"

Scott pulled me up and the world tilted under my feet, but then my back was slamming into the wall and Scott was on me, hands on my hips, mouth biting into mine. It was a hard, desperate kiss, and exactly what I needed.

My fingers went into his hair so I could pull him closer, and then his knee was knocking between mine, pushing his thigh up so I had something to roll my hips against. My head stopped spinning, and all that mattered were his hands shoving under my shirt, the taste of alcohol on his tongue, the fact that he was just as demanding as I'd always dreamt he would be.

He pulled away but didn't stay gone long before his mouth went for my neck instead. I kept a hold on his hair, wrapped my other arm around his back and dug my fingers in. I fell apart when he bit down on my collarbone, and a whispered *'fuck'* sounded like relief and a curse at the same time.

He was the King of Bad Ideas, but I'd never been known for sticking to things that were good for me.

6
"WE SHOULD FORM A SUPPORT GROUP."

"Mornings are awful."

"You're only saying that because you never sleep." Rick patted the top of my head and I did my best to slap him away but I was too damn tired to get my point across.

I'd managed to make it to the table for breakfast, but only long enough to pillow my head in my arms and declare my hatred for everyone who decided being up before 8AM was a good idea. "Like that's bad reasoning," I muttered.

"Still not sleeping?" Juliet asked as she sat across from me and handed over a bowl of cereal. Chocolate milk and everything. I'd call her a goddess, except she ate hers dry, like some kind of heathen.

"I sleep," I said. She shot me a look. "Pass out. Same difference."

"It's really not," Rick argued.

"Aren't you supposed to be at work?" I snapped at him.

"Aren't you supposed to be at school?"

"Breakfast is the most important part of the day," Juliet said. "Plus, we'll make it in time. Dad gave me my keys back."

I was going to die. If riding in a car with Juliet driving didn't do me in, the kids at school definitely would. I sighed and focused on my cereal while Rick and Juliet talked. I was sure I nodded off, because she had to tap the table in front of me to tell me it was time to go.

I tried at least three times on the way to convince her that skipping would be cool, but she wasn't buying it. I groaned, sank down in my seat, and silently moped about the fact that my school uniform didn't come with a hood that I could hide away in.

"You're going to be fine," Juliet said as she pulled into the parking lot. I highly doubted that.

"You're only saying that because you actually have friends," I grumbled.

Juliet didn't reply while she got out of the car. I followed her, but I wasn't happy about it.

It was still daunting to see the Bridgewood Academy High School building and be a part of it. It was much bigger than the Middle School or Elementary, and the architecture was obviously done up in a proud way that said 'our parents have too much money, that's why we go here.'

"Hell," I said. "We're entering hell."

Juliet's nose scrunched up and I knew she wasn't going to argue with me. At least with the uniforms I faded into the crowd instead of sticking out, even with my long sleeves.

We stopped by the Vice Principal's office to pick up our schedules, and the woman took a moment to outline mine. I'd almost managed to skip ninth grade altogether, and my AP courses put me in a lot of sophomore classes, but I was behind in social studies and foreign languages, which hadn't been offered the year before.

Unfortunately, I didn't have a lot of classes with Juliet, but I got her for French and Art. I refused to think about how many classes I would end up sharing with Scott. I knew he wasn't exceeding expectations as far as his coursework went, so there would likely be a lot, but I also knew obsessing over it would only lead to trouble.

It was my fucking first day, I had no room for Scott White in my head.

Juliet gave me a quick tour, then left me on my own as she ran off to homeroom. I sighed, hitched my bag up farther on my shoulder, and realized I was going to have to learn how to stand by myself again.

God, I hated life.

I managed to make it to English before the room was completely full, and got the teacher's attention long enough to pass on my Advanced Placement slip. She looked it over, handed it back, and that was when I saw him.

Fucking Scott. In the center of the farthest right row, lounging back in his desk, laughing already. It was too damn early to look that good, especially in a uniform. Some girl I vaguely recognized from the volleyball team was perched on his desk, Matt was sitting directly beside him, and everyone within a five-foot radius was completely zoned in on whatever he was talking about.

He looked up at me once, twice, then smiled before going back to his conversation. My heart stuttered pathetically in my chest, and I reminded myself that I'd known Scott wouldn't hang out with me at school.

I was a gay freshman, for crying out loud. Not to mention I had no desire to be surrounded by that many people all day. It was fine. I was fine. I was not disappointed.

I picked a desk at the back to throw my bag down on, somewhere in the corner so I could minimize contact with other human beings, and settled into what I was sure would be an epically horrible day.

Algebra II started almost the same way, except the teacher demanded that any advanced students sit up front, which was annoying because it turned everyone's attention to us. Someone muttered "nerds," there were five minutes of laughter, and half the class was wasted trying to get everyone on track.

Scott sat in the back. I hated him for picking somewhere I couldn't stare at him.

Third period I had World History, which was a freshman class. I'd seen most of my grade group when I took my finals, but being with them again was weirder than even being back at school. The whispers started up when I sat down, and I wasn't surprised at all that it was Duncan Mann who showed up at my desk, an unattractive sneer on his face.

"I heard you got AIDS, that's where you disappeared off to."

"I heard you have syphilis," I shot back. "Maybe we should form a support group."

There were a few onlookers who appreciated my sass, if the 'oooh's were anything to go off of. Duncan's face went three different shades of red as he pointed a finger at me. "Shut your mouth, homo, before I break your jaw."

I arched an eyebrow slowly. "Well, since we're both in the practice of believing rumors, I'm going to go ahead and say I highly doubt *that* —" I dropped my gaze purposefully to his crotch "— is big enough for the job."

There was another round of responses and when he looked like he was going to deck me right then and there, I tilted my head up to make it easier. I wasn't a fan of getting hit, but if anyone knew how to take a punch, it was me.

Thankfully, the sad excuse of a teacher grabbed everyone's attention then, and Duncan was forced to leave me alone until another day.

I had study hall after that, which wasn't in the freshman curriculum, so I didn't have to deal with anyone or their bullshit for a full forty-five minutes.

Then lunch came.

Despite my dislike for nature in general, I hated cafeterias more. Bridgewood Academy was an open campus, but I had no desire to leave. Instead, I grabbed a tray and went outside. I wasn't the only one, and plenty of groups were scattered about, basking in the sunshine and laughing loudly.

I picked a shady spot by the stairs, popped my headphones in, and tried not to think too hard about anything, like life or that I really, really wanted to be dead.

It worked for about three minutes, then someone had a grip on my arm and was jerking me up. My stomach flipped and instinct brought me to my feet, head spinning and vision threatening to go black. My mind was already telling me that 'yes sir' and 'I'm sorry' were the right things to say, though I bit down on my tongue to keep from doing it.

Duncan ripped my headphones out, pushed me back against the brick wall, my feet stumbled over my fallen food. Gross.

"Seriously?" I snapped. "Are we twelve?"

"Shut up!" Duncan yelled back, and when I tried to take a step away from the wall he pushed me into it again. "You think you can just say that shit to me and walk away?"

I rolled my eyes. "Grow a pair, would you?"

The moment the words left my mouth, pain shot through my jaw and deep into the bone. I mentally cursed myself for not being fast enough to fucking duck.

Before I realized it, I had launched myself at him, catching him around the middle and sending us both to the ground. His friends were cheering, somewhere a girl screamed, but all I cared about were the fists slamming into my sides.

At least until there were hands under my arms, jerking me up. I aimed another desperate kick and caught Duncan in the knee hard enough that he yelled. Damn right.

The jerk's older brother, Douglas, showed up out of nowhere and helped him off the ground, looking about as pissed as I felt. "Are you kidding me?" he was asking. "Were you seriously losing to that queer?"

"The fuck did you just say?" Matt demanded, and I hadn't even realized it was him who had pulled me off until suddenly he was pushing me aside and crossing the distance between us and the brothers.

"You heard me," Douglas said, letting Duncan go and facing Matt head-on. "If you gotta problem you can say it." Douglas had a year on Matt, but Matt had him beat in the muscle department.

It would be an interesting fight, except Kaitlynn stepped in from the sidelines, hands on her hips. "Boys, seriously? Calm your testosterone fueled asses down. If you get caught fighting on the first freaking day of school you'll both end up benched. Get it together."

They stared each other down before Douglas eventually shot a look at me. "Keep your dirty hands off of him."

"Doug, I swear to god," Matt warned, but I was already talking ahead of him: "Don't worry, pussies aren't my thing."

Douglas took an angry step toward me and Matt moved right in his path. It pissed me off, but I had to admit Douglas could probably aim one good push at me and I'd go down. He drew up short, Matt was too big for him to take on face to face. He'd probably just talk shit about him later.

"Hey!" Kaitlynn snapped. "Let it go!"

She stormed across the small area to get ahold of Douglas herself, nudging him out of the ring of onlookers. Duncan followed behind them with his head dropped in shame and fists still clenched. I pressed two fingers to the right side of my aching jaw and winced.

Matt looked back at me and the corners of his mouth twitched into a smile. "Lakyn, you are such a little shit."

"That's what they tell me," I muttered, and noticed Scott, who was holding a bag of take-out chicken and a tray of drinks.

"What the hell did I miss?" he asked.

Matt ruffled my hair in a brotherly fashion before throwing an arm over my shoulders. "This jerk is fighting on the first day."

Scott's eyebrows went up. "Really?"

As usual, his entourage jumped to attention, everyone ready with slightly different accounts of what had gone down. Scott listened to a few of them before shaking the bag of food in my direction. "Want some chicken?"

My heart skipped. Over chicken. Fuck.

I told it to shut up and shook my head while I moved out from under Matt's arm. "Nah. I'm fine."

Scott's gaze dropped to the food I'd crushed when Duncan had decided to be an asshole, but I held my ground with a glare. "I'm fine, Scott."

He shrugged, Matt clapped my shoulder, and they left me alone. I watched them go before heading back inside to the library while I waited for lunch to be over, then I went to Art.

"The hell happened to you?" was the first thing Juliet said to me when I walked in. She was sitting with her friend Romilda, who had a pixie cut, a nose ring, and liked to test the limits of the dress code. I wasn't fond of her, but I was fond of Juliet, so I took a seat by them anyway. Her fingers went under my chin so she could tilt my head to the side, and she frowned at the bruise forming on my jaw. "Dad's not going to be happy."

"Well, he can't stop teenagers from being assholes, can he?" I said.

"Tell me you won?" Romilda asked, glancing at me boredly while she picked at the dark polish on her nails. "It's only sexy if you won."

I shrugged and she shook her head, deciding I wasn't worth her time. Juliet gave me a look but I nudged her shoulder with mine as a sign not to worry about it. We both knew I could handle much, much worse.

The art teacher started on a 'tell us about you' piece. Romilda opened her sketchbook, flipped to a random page, pulled the gum out of her mouth and smeared it from one corner to the other. "I call it: A Day in my Mouth."

Juliet laughed. I didn't.

I wasn't very artistic, but I liked working with my hands, so I made a couple of random patterns and colored them with dark shades. It did the job, and then I was off to sophomore Chemistry.

It was another one of those annoying as hell set-ups, because the lab tables were made for pairs. Scott and Matt were already taking over one of the middle ones, and Matt grabbed my arm as I passed by. I went tense, and he shot a look at Scott before glancing at me again.

"Sit with Jason," Scott said, nodding his head toward the kid at the table in front of them. He was alone thus far, arms crossed, body language daring anyone to mess with him.

"Are you making decisions for me now?" I asked.

"Trying to keep you out of detention, maybe?" Matt offered.

"Or off suicide watch," Scott whispered. I glared at him, and Matt either didn't hear or did a good job of pretending not to.

"Leave me alone." I pulled out of Matt's grasp, surveyed the room as a whole, sighed and backtracked to where Jason was. I knew him by association, and I knew he had declared back in middle school that he was going to be Valedictorian. No one had argued. "Can I sit here?"

"AP?" he asked and when I nodded he continued with, "Don't distract me."

"Wouldn't dare," I answered, and proceeded not to say a word for the rest of the class.

I had French with Juliet after that. Aunt Lily's parents lived in France, so she'd picked up the language pretty fluently. She'd taught both Rick and Juliet when they were children, claiming it was a skill that would be useful for them one day. I knew a good portion of it myself, so I wouldn't fail at least.

None of Juliet's friends took Art, which meant I got her full attention. She was more herself without them around, although I had a feeling she was at least slightly high. After that was General PE, with a coach who showed off her new engagement ring and then left everyone alone to do wedding planning on her laptop.

I changed out and decided to run a couple of laps around the gym. Thanks to my summer with Scott I could push five more out of myself than the last time I'd been there. I missed the days of physically running away from my problems, it'd been a less painful coping mechanism than the cutting. I'd only quit because I'd been too damn tired to do anything. Like live.

Scott found me in the hallway afterwards, still in his workout jersey and shorts, wet hair pushed back. I ignored him while I got my locker open to grab my books.

"How was it?" he asked gently.

I sighed. "I'm not going to go home and swallow a bunch of pills, if that's what you're asking."

He was quiet long enough that I took the chance to glance at him. He was staring at his feet instead of me, his fingers tapping against the metal lockers in a slow, uncomfortable pattern. I was sure he was remembering the scars on my wrists, likely wondering if I was joking when things like that came out of my mouth. Finally, he looked up, and his usual fucking bright-ass smile was back in place. "So, when did you start fighting?"

"Go away."

"C'mon, I gotta know. How many moves do you have? Did you take a class or is it pure street —"

"Get off my dick, Scott," I complained, slamming my locker door shut.

"Now, that would be completely counterproductive to my seduction plan," Scott muttered. When I looked back he had a full pout in place, eyes wide and innocent.

I laughed despite myself. "You're such a fucking nerd."

He grinned. "You like it."

"True. But you have boundary issues," I stated, and immediately his expression fell. We hadn't talked since the incident at his party, and I knew that was what was on his mind. He ran a hand through his hair and I tried not to get distracted by the way his muscles worked. It wasn't easy.

"If you really want me to back off, I will," he said, with complete sincerity. "Give me a solid no. Right now. No hurt feelings, no arguments. I'll walk away. I'll leave you alone."

"I don't want you to stop," I admitted. That wasn't easy either.

His eyebrows shot up, and I shook my head slowly. "Wanna fuck?" I asked.

He reeled back, but got over his surprise quickly. "Doesn't your jaw hurt?"

I shrugged. "Yours doesn't."

He smirked at me and I nodded before spinning around and walking off ahead of him. I caught Juliet's gaze on the way out and gestured at Scott to let her know I had a ride. She looked amused, waved in a way that said she knew what I was getting up to, and headed toward her car alone.

7
"NO CUTS, NO DRINKS."

Scott's bedroom door slammed shut in one moment, and in the next my back was pressed against it, wrists locked in his hands and pinned above my head. His teeth sank into my lower lip and the small stab of pain sent a shiver up my spine.

"Light," I mumbled against his lips, but I could barely hear it over my own panting. It'd been like that since we'd gotten into the house. All clawing fingers and sharp teeth and tripping out of our shoes. Trying to get at each other. *Now, please, more.* God, *please* more. "Scott."

"What?" he whispered, breath fanning against my neck before his tongue took its place, dragging from my collarbone to the spot just behind my ear. My fists clenched in on themselves; a desperate need to hold onto something, but he wasn't letting go.

"Off," I said, trying to explain, but his teeth were digging into the skin just before my shoulder and all the blood in my brain decided it had fucking better places to be. He felt too damn *good*.

He finally released my hands, letting me drop my arms around his neck, so that I could pull his mouth back to mine. He kissed like he *meant it*, and I barely noticed his fingers working at the buttons on my shirt. He pushed it open but I didn't care, not when his body was so warm against mine. I wanted more, so much so that I was shaking by the time his hands were running down my rib cage. Bare skin against bare skin, his tongue in my mouth. *Please.*

His fingers paused in their path and I opened my eyes in irritation. His gaze had locked onto the exposed skin of my torso as he lifted the edges of my shirt to see better. I licked my lips slowly as I felt his touch graze over whichever scar had caught his attention, where the waist of my pants weren't quite high enough to cover.

His gaze shifted to my face again, and I felt myself bracing for this to be over. For him to ask questions, pass judgment, shake his head and step away. I didn't know what surprised me more: when he didn't look at me any differently, or when he slid his fingers into a belt loop so he could tug me off the door and get the rest of my shirt off.

It fell to the ground before he was following the light scars across my shoulders and biceps with gentle fingertips, taking my left hand in both of his and turning it to see the pale lines it was decorated with.

His thumb grazed the cut that had almost taken my life, the movement slow, like he was memorizing the mark. Temporarily satisfied with his observations, his mouth found mine again while his shoulders pressed me back into the door.

His fingers were busy working the button and zipper on my pants, struggling only for a few seconds before his lips moved to my throat. Chest. Stomach. Navel.

He sunk to his knees as he traveled downward. My fucking heart betrayed me, skipping a couple of beats as I forced out his name. "*Scott.*"

His mouth was tracing the scars on both sides of my hips — soft, tender, caring — while the air escaping his nose tickled teasingly against my skin. My mind scrambled as I tried to figure out what the fuck I was feeling while his touch distracted any attempt at concentration. Nervousness? Excitement? He was too goddamn soft with me and I just couldn't — No one was ever soft with me.

He worked my pants down centimeter by centimeter, building me up and slowly, *slowly* tearing me apart. The friction was unbelievable, but only prolonged what I needed from him.

I swallowed thickly, eyes falling to watch him like maybe he'd do me the favor of seeming as fucking into it as I was. I knew he had to be.

More scars. More kisses.

His fingers moved along the line of my boxers slowly, dipping under the elastic before he gave a slight tug. He was asking for permission, but my mind was on a mission to short-circuit.

"*Fuck,*" I breathed out, head dropping back with the knowledge that my voice had cracked. I should have been embarrassed, but it would come later. If at all.

We were doing this.

My fingers unfurled from their fists and sank into his hair instead, breathing so damn hard I figured I'd pass out, holding on because I knew he could destroy me if he wanted.

"You better be fucking good at this," I muttered.

Scott nipped at my hip in warning, earning an airy chuckle from me — a sound that broke into a pleading whimper the moment his fingers slid through the coarse patch of hair that lead to the base of my dick. Target in sight and suddenly I didn't feel so worried anymore. "Scott."

He took his sweet fucking time, waiting until pleas were begging to be released from the tip of my tongue, before he pushed my boxers out of the way and took me into his mouth, wrapping his hand around what he couldn't fit.

My mind blanked out in one second of pleasure, jaw dropping and fingers gripping too tightly at his hair. I couldn't fucking *breathe*. It was so warm. So perfect.

"Is that good enough for you?" Scott mumbled when he took a break, and my face dropped down toward him long enough to glare. He met my gaze with a smirk as he dragged his tongue slowly from base to tip. Holy fuck.

"I. Hate. You," I ground out between clenched teeth.

"Mmhmm," Scott replied easily, following the path his tongue had made with his palm. Just the right amount of pressure. Just the right twist at the end. "We'll see how long that lasts."

His lips slid back over my dick before I could retort and I bit off a curse, closing my eyes and holding onto him again. His pace was perfect. He was perfect.

My hips jerked unsteadily and his free hand pressed against my thigh, holding me down. Too soon I could feel the build-up, the need to curl my toes and pull him off. "Scott, Scott, Scott," I warned, tugging at his hair. I couldn't take it anymore. It'd been too damn long and he was too damn good.

He pulled away and replaced his mouth with his hand, stroking fast enough to

urge me toward the finish. I came so hard I saw colors, white hot pleasure flooding my body, and he didn't let up. Kept going at it until I was shaking and begging for some relief. My knees buckled and met the floor, collapsing to the ground right in front of him.

He caught me, of fucking course he did, right against his chest, pressing his lips to my temple before letting me rest against the door.

I watched him lick his lips and reached out to press my thumb to the corner of his mouth. I was lightheaded and tired, but I still felt the need to touch him.

He grinned at me like an idiot.

"Mm." I slid my hand to his shirt and curled my fist into the pressed cotton. "Why are you still wearing clothes?"

"I don't know," Scott answered like the smartass he was. "Why *am I* still wearing clothes?"

"I'm too tired to deal with you," I said, and didn't even bother to close the last inch between us for a kiss. Instead I dropped my hand and glared. "Take care of that, would you?"

Scott stood up, working the buttons on his shirt slowly before pulling it off. His skin was still summer tanned, muscles still toned and perfect. He went for his pants next; buttons, zip, dark red boxer shorts obviously strained. My mouth was wet suddenly, nerves on fire again. He pulled them both down, and damn.

Damn.

"Lube?"

Scott ran his hands through his hair before turning to his nightstand. He found what he was looking for, but hesitated.

I knew why, instantly.

"Scott," I muttered, and his head turned toward me out of habit. "You're fine."

He didn't look convinced, so I switched tactics. "If I can make it without the lights off, you can make it without a damn drink. Now are you gonna let me jerk you off or not?"

He let out a low chuckle as he walked back over to me, dropping the bottle in my lap and bracing his hands against the door. I grinned and poured a generous amount in my palm before finally, *finally* getting my hand around Scott White's junk.

"Lakyn," he murmured, and I glanced up just in time to see his eyes shut.

I couldn't wait to watch him fall apart.

***

I was half asleep when I felt Scott's fingers on my wrist, tracing the scars there lightly. "You do this all the time," he said. "What are you thinking about?"

I sighed and tucked my free arm under my head, resisting the urge to jerk the sheet up so I could hide. It was pooled around my waist, but I felt way too exposed suddenly. "Scott —"

"You think about how you're supposed to be dead, don't you?"

I stared at the ceiling instead of answering, but Scott didn't seem to mind. His fingers moved from that scar to the others, going up my arm to my shoulder. Finally I said, "Usually, yeah."

"Why so many different places?" he asked, sliding down the bed slightly so that he could lie next to me, resting his head against my chest. His touch went to my hips instead, where the scars were longer and easier to reach.

"They're all for different things," I answered.

"Tell me about them?"

I licked my lips and moved my arm from under my head to wrap around him instead, my hand resting against the base of his neck so I could slide my fingers through the short hair there. It wouldn't be easy to talk about.

"Um, the ones on my biceps are for when I'm really stressed out or panicking. And uh, the ones on my thighs are, like, sometimes I feel numb.

Like I'm detached from the world? It's really unsettling, and the skin there is tender, so it pulls me back faster."

I took a deep breath. These were things I hadn't told anyone. Things that I was supposed to tell my therapist but that felt too personal to bring up or let go of. But this was Scott. "My hips are for when I regret things because, if I think about stuff too much I can make myself physically sick. For days, even, if it's bad enough. And, um…"

"Your wrists," Scott muttered, when I couldn't bring myself to say it. "Are for when you don't want to live anymore?"

I let out a breath and didn't have to answer, because we both knew he was right. We sat in silence, the rhythmic feeling of his fingers moving against my skin more soothing than words could ever be.

"What does it feel like?" he asked.

"Cutting?" I said, and he nodded his head against me slightly. "I don't know. It's hard to explain. Like 'control,' kind of, like 'reality.' It feels like something is pushing right against the surface, and it hurts, and if you can just open that surface up and let it out, it'll be better."

"Is it?" Scott asked. "Better?"

"No," I admitted, and felt a weight settle against my chest over it. I knew it wasn't healthy, I knew it wasn't fixing anything, I just couldn't stop myself. "Maybe for a while, but then the pain comes back."

I expected him to ask me why I did it. To berate me, or tell me I was dumb, or that I had enough mental scars and I didn't really need to add more physical ones. All of which were valid points, I just knew I couldn't handle hearing them.

Not from him.

Instead, he tilted his head back to look at me and raised his fingers to my bruised jaw. "Does it hurt?"

"Little bit," I answered with a wince. "Probably should have iced it instead of, well, doing all this."

He chuckled then yawned, his thumb moving gently over my bottom lip before dropping against my shoulder. "Probably. Regrets?"

I thought about that, thought about the cuts on my hips, but in the end, I shook my head. "No. No regrets."

"Good," Scott murmured, finally starting to sound as exhausted as I felt. "You can stay the night, if you want. My parents won't be home until tomorrow afternoon."

"Nah," I said, and ran my fingers through his hair before tugging him away from me. "My uncle will come looking for me eventually."

Scott nodded and let me up, and I stretched out my sore muscles before turning back to him. I leaned over for a kiss. "Try not to drink yourself to sleep tonight, okay?"

"No cuts, no drinks," he offered.

"No cuts, no drinks."

***

Scott made himself a cup of coffee before driving me home and didn't even complain when I drank half of it. There was no goodbye kiss, but he did smile, soft and sweet. I wanted to tell him to cut it out, but it felt good.

"See you tomorrow," I said in way of parting, grabbing my bag off the floor of his Jeep.

"Eat lunch with us," Scott requested, folding his arms over the wheel. "I know it's a lot of people, but, please."

"Why do we always end up having this conversation?" I mumbled. "You don't want me there, Scott. You know you don't."

"Do you know what I did all day today?" Scott asked. "I thought about you. And how your day was going. And where you were. And I volunteered to pick up everyone's food so I could get away from you and breathe just for a little while, but all I could really think about was the fact that you could've been there with me, so —"

I knew I must have been giving him a look, because his mouth shut suddenly and the slightest shade of pink touched his cheeks. He cleared his throat and looked away. "Post-sex talking."

"No it's not," I accused. "But you're talking like someone who wants a boyfriend, Scott."

"Doesn't matter," he said. "You don't do boyfriends."

"I don't do sex with my friends either and yet here we are," I shot back. His head snapped around toward me, eyes slightly wide, and I shrugged. "So, are we good, just doing what we're doing?"

"Would you want more?"

"Would you want to come out?" I asked, and his wince was all the answer I needed. I sighed and sat back against the seat. "I'm not saying you have to. Come out when you're ready. But the second we label this as something important, it's going to come with boyfriend perks. And I... I could *want* those with you. I could want to hold your hand in the hall and kiss you goodbye every day. I'm not even sure I'm ready for that, I don't date for a reason, but that's what happens. And I can admit that I could want it."

"Okay," Scott answered after a pause. "But if we keep doing what we're doing?"

"Then it's just for fun." I shrugged. "We're just friends who hang out and suck each other's dick instead of playing video games."

He tilted his head in thought. "We should play video games sometimes."

I laughed. "Refractory periods are a thing."

Finally, his face broke into one of those stupid, stupid grins. "So, about school?"

"I'll hang out with you if you want me to. But you've got to be prepared to deal with the shit it gets you, Scott. Because, as we've just discussed, I can't hold your hand through it. That's a boyfriend perk, and we don't get those."

Scott nodded and I repeated the gesture before finally getting out of the Jeep. I turned back before I shut the door, aware by his mood that his emotions were frayed. "You okay?"

He smiled and nodded, but it wasn't right.

"No cuts," I promised.

"No drinks," he said.

"Just don't give yourself alcohol poisoning, alright?" I shut the door that time and watched him drive off, still feeling his mouth on mine. Holding me together. Pulling me apart. I felt calmer than I had in a while.

My uncle was in the living room working on his laptop, but he looked up when I crossed his path. "Hey, Jules said you went to Scott's after school. Did you have a good day — what happened to your face?"

"Huh?" I asked, then my fingers raised to the bruise that had spread across my jawline. I winced at the way he studied me. "Uh, I don't guess the 'I ran into a door' excuse still works, does it?"

He was so horribly unamused that I felt chastised without him saying anything. "It's no big deal. I just got into a little fight at lunch. It's fine."

"Lakyn."

"It's *fine*," I stressed.

Uncle Ben sighed and pinched at the bridge of his nose, obviously deciding how much he wanted to put up with from me. "Who threw the first punch?"

"He did," I said, and tapped my fingers lightly over the discolored patch of skin. "I just went for defense, and then we got broken up. It really wasn't a big deal."

He didn't look like he believed me at all, but he finally nodded. "Well, it's something you should probably bring up with Frank. And if it keeps happening it's something *I* will bring up with your school. There's pizza in the kitchen."

"Okay," I said, and dropped my bag and shoes off by the door. "Uncle Ben?"

"Yeah?"

"All things considered, it was a good day."

His smile was one of relief and he went back to his work without any more pushing, so I left him alone to go grab a couple of slices of pizza. Juliet was there, sitting on the edge of the counter and typing away on her phone. She grinned at me and I flipped her off without looking.

"You smell like sex and sweat and bad ideas," she stated.

"I don't know what you're talking about," I murmured.

Juliet hummed in a way that let me know she was aware I was full of shit. "I didn't know Scott knew he was gay."

I looked up at her and pointedly raised an eyebrow.

"*Come on*, Lakyn, I hung out with you guys this summer. Anyone that's not blind can tell he's into you. Like, a lot."

"Anyone with rainbow glasses, maybe," I said as I leaned my hip against the counter she was sitting on. "I think Kaitlynn's pretty sure Scott's straight enough that my queerness isn't a threat to her gigantic crush on him, but we'll see if that lasts."

"Mm, you're a threat alright," Juliet decided, leaning over to pull a pepperoni off one of my pizza slices. "So, how was he?"

I snorted. "I'm not going to give you details."

"I didn't ask for details, you little whore. I'm just curious."

I smiled as I bit into an extra cheesy slice. Scott had worn me out, but I still had the memory of him on me. "Amazing. He was amazing."

"You're so bad," she said.

"Like you're not."

She shrugged and slid off the counter, then picked up both our plates. "Wanna go smoke?"

"Yeah," I answered, needing something to take the Scott edge off. "Just don't let me fall asleep, I need a shower."

"Yeah, you do," Juliet muttered, and laughed when I shoved her for it.

.

8
"I HAVE SIXTEEN YEARS WORTH OF ISSUES STACKED UP."

"I think, at this point, Lakyn and I have done all we can together."

The room fell silent after Frank spoke. He sat patiently in front of us, his hands resting on my file, waiting on a response. My uncle shifted in his seat next to me. "So, what you're saying is?"

"I no longer believe I can help him," Frank stated. "I think he would be better off in someone else's care. I have a list of recommendations here —"

I pushed myself off the couch and started for the door. Uncle Ben called my name but I didn't bother turning back around. "Keep your bullshit list," I muttered, shouldering my way out of the room.

I didn't sign out with the receptionist, almost tripped over a kid playing with a toy airplane, but finally made it outside. Not that it was much better there, because it was still too damn warm, but at least it was quiet.

I sighed as I sank to the curb, pushing my fingers up under my sleeve so that I could trace at a well-memorized scar. It'd been a long week, although better than I'd expected. After the first day of school I'd had less problems. My AP courses kept me with mostly sophomores, and although some of them were dicks, they generally didn't care about who I was or my drama. Likewise, the upperclassmen didn't care, because I was too 'young' to be on their radar. The only real problem came from the other freshmen, but I only saw them once a day.

Duncan had decided to keep his distance, but Matt let me know the kick I'd aimed at his knee had taken him out of athletics for the week. I was oddly proud of that fact, and filed it away for later use in case the bitchass decided to open his mouth again.

Besides a few shoves in the hallway and a couple of books slapped out of my hands, people left me alone. It was a cakewalk compared to the year before.

Scott didn't let up about me hanging out with him during lunch though. The first few days were awkward as hell, but then a pattern set in. There were a few odd looks on occasion, but apparently Scott was cool enough that no one questioned his judgment. At least, they hadn't yet. I was sure it would happen eventually. It wasn't particularly my idea of fun, but it wasn't a bad way to spend half an hour every day.

I dug my fingernails into the ruined skin of my wrist, waiting for the slight pinch of pain. This was it. This was my life. It was moving on like nothing had happened. As easily and involuntarily as breathing or my heart beating. Things most people found amazing when they actually sat back and noticed them, but I'd long ago become disillusioned to.

Usually I was just annoyed.

I pulled my phone out to text Scott and ask if his parents were home. He replied that they were, but we could still hang out. I told him it was fine and dropped my head into my hands, pressing my palms against my eyes. The last thing I needed was to start relying on Scott like a coping mechanism, even if he proved a particularly useful one. He was already a bad idea, but couldn't let him become a bad habit.

The door opened and closed behind me. I didn't have to look up to know it was my uncle. "You okay?"

"Peachy," I answered.

"I wasn't aware you liked Frank that much."

"I don't." I pulled my face out of my hands to glance up at him. He had that same slightly worried look in his eye he always had when he focused on me. It was bothersome, but I understood where it came from. "But I'm so fucking sick of people giving up on me."

It was such a rare moment of vulnerable honesty that Uncle Ben's expression crumpled. He sat down next to me and shook his head. "I'm not giving up on you," he said, and when I didn't have a reply for him, he emphasized it. "*Lakyn*, I'm not. But this is part of you not giving up on yourself, okay? This is something you've got to do. You've got to talk to someone, because there are things I can't help you with. Not because I don't want to, but because I don't know how. You get that, right?"

"I'm difficult," I said. "I'm defensive, and sarcastic, and apathetic. I have sixteen years worth of issues stacked up and trust me, I'm used to getting broken. You get that, right?"

He chuckled and looped an arm around my neck, pulling me into an easy headlock. He'd done it a lot when I was a kid, and it'd never scared me. *He'd* never scared me. "I know. We'll figure this out, kid."

"Yeah." I sighed, and when his grip loosened I let myself sit there for just a bit longer, soaking up the warmth and the comfort of someone who believed I was going to be okay, even if it took some time. "I don't want his damn list though. If we're starting over, we're starting over. Completely."

"Alright." He stood up first and held a hand down to me. I took it and let him pull me up, and tried to remember that I didn't have to do things alone anymore.

***

The second Saturday into the school year I found myself at some party that was more sleazy than it was fun. I wasn't even sure whose house we were in, although I had a feeling it was a senior's. The party spilled from the ground floor to the basement, the music was way too loud, and the alcohol was strong.

Scott was to blame, as usual. I'd been hanging out with him and Matt when they got the text, and after a brief conversation it was decided that going to the party would be better than smoking in Matt's backyard, which had been the plan.

When I'd said I'd just go home and do some schoolwork, Scott had turned that damn puppy dog look on me until I'd caved.

Now I couldn't even find the bastard.

Getting down the steps into the basement was a bitch and a half, because for whatever reason, everyone had decided to hang out on them. It was the darkest area in the house, which was dangerous as hell, and apparently the perfect place to hook up. I was ninety percent sure I saw at least three hand-jobs and stepped over a couple going the full third base, but I didn't try to look closer.

Downstairs was where most of the guys had gathered. The music was loud, the few girls were beyond drunk, and I sighed as I started nudging my way through the grinding bodies, holding my drink up in the air so hopefully it wouldn't spill down my shirt if someone decided to ram into me.

I had a nice buzz going on, which was doing a good job of distracting me from the shit in my head. I'd spent a fair amount of time during the last few weeks on some substance or another, thanks to the turmoil of trying to find a new therapist.

It wasn't fun.

Neither was this, though.

Somewhere in the center of the room, everyone's attention was turned inwards, cheers carried over the thumping bass, and I had to lift up onto my toes before I realized what had caught everyone's attention. Girls, dancing all up on each other. There were hands on hips that were mostly bare due to low waistlines, and mouths that were almost touching. Almost, but not quite, teasing every stereotypical male that had ever watched girl on girl porn in his life. It was a live show.

It was *Juliet*.

She was with Stella Wilson, who had been expelled from BA a year ago. Something to do with trespassing or drugs in her locker, I didn't quite remember. Juliet had been friends with her younger sister back in middle school, but I wasn't aware she knew Stella that well.

When they finally kissed, the crowd went wild, and my stomach flipped as they just fucking *went for it*. Stella's hands were up Juliet's shirt, and Juliet's hands went down the back of her skirt, dragging her in closer. It was dirty and intense and not like my cousin at all.

Someone pulled a phone out and I finally jerked into motion, pushing my way into the break between the people and the girls.

"Hey, hey!" I snapped before putting a hand on Juliet's arm. She pulled away from Stella but didn't let her go, just turned her head toward me. Even in the dim lighting, I could tell she wasn't all there. Her gaze couldn't stay focused, and the smile on her face wasn't her own.

"Lakyn! Wassup, cuz?" she said with a grin, then leaned so heavily into Stella they both nearly fell. The girls giggled, and Stella moved her hands off my cousin's boobs to wrap her arms around her waist.

"I think you've had enough," I tried, feeling out of my element. I wasn't anyone's care-taker, I could barely look after myself, and the music meant I had to yell at her. There was no way to do anything privately or with care, but I couldn't just leave her like that.

"Enough what?" she asked, blinking slow, red-rimmed eyes at me. I made a general gesture over her and Stella's intertwined bodies to mean *all of this*, but before I could say anything else, some douche canoe from the crowd had shown up, dropping an arm around Stella and Juliet's shoulders and putting himself in the middle of them. Juliet was gone enough she didn't seem to notice the switch, but Stella did, and I felt my nose scrunch up as she stuck her *tongue* in his *ear*.

What the hell.

"Hey buddy," the guy said. He was too old for me to know him, probably a senior, or a graduated perv. "Why don't you fuck off, huh? Who are you, anyway?"

The message was clear: *'these girls are mine for the night, so go before I make you go.'* I was in over my head, but I felt my teeth clench anyway. I'd take a hit if it meant I could get her out. I didn't like the situation at all.

"Mine," Juliet answered for me, her fingers clumsily reaching for my wrist. Once, twice, before I felt bad enough to just give her my hand. She couldn't find the word for 'cousin' and kept stumbling: "He's my, my, um. Mine."

Douche Canoe's eyebrows drew down in confusion, like he couldn't decide why anyone who looked like her would want anything to do with *me*. "I just wanna take her home, alright man?" I asked, just in case I could give him the benefit of being a decent fucking person underneath it all.

He looked between Juliet and Stella, both of whom were still tucked under his arms, though Juliet still didn't seem to understand that at all. She was leaning on him, but I had a feeling it was more because she couldn't stand on her own.

"Nah. The girls are just having a little fun, right, ladies? I think they'd rather be with me."

I felt sick and Stella gave me a grin before leaning over and pinching my cheek between her fingers. I jerked back and slapped her hand away harder than I'd intended, but the bitch just leered at me. "Feisty," she commented. "I like it. Wanna stay and play?"

"No." I twisted my hand around in Juliet's until I could get an actual grip on her, then tugged. She stumbled toward me, but the asshole's hand dropped to her hip and pulled her back. He had half a foot on me at least, and probably two or three times the muscle. Bigger than the last guy I'd gotten into a fight with, but not as big as my father. I could take a hit from him, I'd be fine. "Let her go."

The guy gave me a nasty grin as he leaned down between the girls to get on my level. "You know, I don't think I will."

Big mistake. I dropped my drink and slammed my fist into his nose. It *hurt*, my knuckles protested and a shock traveled up to my elbow, but I didn't have time to think about it. The dude went down, taking Stella with him, but my own hand was still wrapped in Juliet's, so she stayed standing.

"Ouch," she said, but I figured she was talking about the death grip I had on her fingers rather than the dude that was probably holding his face by now. I twisted around and shoved Juliet in front of me. Even drunk — and probably stoned — she understood *move*. She pushed ahead of me through the crowd that was just catching onto what had happened, and I followed her like my damn life depended on it.

Scott was just coming down the staircase when Juliet went past him, and he looked after her like he wasn't sure who he'd just seen, before turning and catching sight of me. That stupid grin covered his face and a greeting was right on the tip of his tongue before I shook my head and skipped the first few steps.

"Run!"

Juliet tripped at least three times, over someone's limbs or the stairs themselves I wasn't sure, I just put my hands on her back and pushed her up again. I was pretty sure she was giggling and apologizing as she stumbled through.

It took a while to get out the front door, because I wasn't even completely sure where it was. I smacked into more people than I managed to dodge, but eventually I got us outside.

The lack of music was a shock to my senses, and the adrenaline seemed to stop dead in its tracks once I was hit with the cool night air and silence.

"*Motherfucker!*" I yelled, bringing my injured hand up to cradle against my chest. It burned, and the skin across my knuckles looked like it was going to bruise.

"What the hell, Lakyn?" Scott demanded, following after us. He still had his drink in his hand somehow, and dark liquid spilled over the top. "Are you trying to fight everyone this year?"

"Just the jerks who have it coming," I muttered under my breath while trying to shake the pain out of my fingers. It was a bad idea and I regretted it immediately.

I knew Scott was about to start in on me, but a yelp caught our attention. Juliet had managed to fall flat on her ass. She looked awful. Most of her mascara was running down her face, her lipstick was smudged, her too-tight crop top was halfway up her bra, and her skinny jeans were covered in spilled drinks.

"Is she okay?" Scott asked.

"Definitely not," I said, and gave up on my hand to squat down in front of her.

"Jules. *Jules*," I repeated, when I couldn't get her attention. "What did you take?"

Immediately defensive, Juliet's expression went dark. "What did *you* take?" she shot back.

It was more than just weed, more than just booze, but I didn't know what. Drugs had never really been my thing, somehow, and while I'd been worried they were hers, it'd never been as strong a feeling as it was now. "I'm trying to help you."

"Help me?" she asked, and I'd never heard that tone in her voice before. "I'm not the one who needs help, Lakyn! *You* are. Because everything's about you, isn't it? You're the only one in this family who gets to be fucked-up, right? I have to be okay, because *you're* not."

That hurt. That hurt worse than my stupid hand, and I took a deep breath as I stared at her. I didn't recognize her, and that was the only thing that kept me grounded. The only thing that kept me from breaking. "Jules," I tried again, but my voice wavered.

"I'm sorry, Lakyn," she stated sarcastically. It was going to get worse. "I'm sorry your dad hit you, and I'm sorry your mom is fucking awful, but I only have one parent left. *One*, do you get that? I shouldn't have to share with you!"

A stupid fucking tear broke free before I could stop it. I swallowed down the lump in my throat and watched her attempt to get up. She made it on the third try, took a few steps away from me, then hit the grass again on her knees before vomiting.

I stood myself and grabbed her arm to pull the band from her wrist before trying to gather all her hair and get it out of the way. When I glanced up to see where Scott had gone, I found him right where I'd left him, expression broken and sad. I couldn't stand that look on him, so I cleared my throat and wiped my eyes with the back of my hand. "Go back to the party."

"Lakyn," he said gently, taking a step toward me. I felt my back go tense in an effort not to back away, and shook my head harshly. *I can't deal with this right now.* He stopped, hands lifted in surrender.

"Go," I said, "I've got this."

He hesitated, one foot poised to do what I said, but the rest of his being was obviously at war with the order. "I —"

"Go!" I was going to start crying again, because I was drunk, and Juliet had clawed through my armor. Scott had seen me naked before, had seen the scars on my body, but this? This was a different sort of vulnerability, and I hadn't been ready to show it to him yet.

He licked his lips nervously. "You don't have a car."

I didn't, and the frustration of that fact almost brought on another wave of tears. I took a deep breath, listening to Juliet dry-heave a couple of times before she finally leaned back against my legs, empty and exhausted.

"How drunk are you?" I asked when I could finally look at Scott again.

"I've only had two," he promised, and tipped over the cup he was holding, spilling out what was left in it. "Didn't get to drink most of that. Spilled it all running after your ass."

I chuckled, a little hysterically, trying to regain some normalcy. "Yeah. You're always running after my ass."

Scott quirked a smile then walked over to help pull Juliet to her feet and not stumble. "Lakyn," she murmured, holding onto him tightly, not realizing we'd switched places. "I want to take a nap."

"Okay," I said, and Scott got her in the back seat of the Jeep before I climbed in after her. I let her rest her head in my lap, and ran my fingers through her hair while Scott drove. It was late, so the roads were mostly empty, but Scott still obeyed the traffic laws anyway.

It didn't take long to get home, and Scott carried Juliet inside. We shed our shoes by the door and he laid her on the bed, but loitered outside her room while I took care of her. She was groggy, but helped me trade her top with an oversized T-shirt, and managed to get her pants mostly off after I took care of her shoes.

She passed out as soon as her head hit the pillow, and I shut her bedroom door softly as I left. Silently, Scott and I walked back outside, and I sighed as we sat down on the front porch.

Scott pulled a joint from his pocket and offered it to me. I considered telling him no, but I was pulled so thin that I knew it was either going to be lighting up, or taking a blade to my skin once I got back to my own room. "Thanks," I muttered.

There was silence and smoke, and I kept the joint to myself because I knew Scott would have to drive home. He didn't ask for it either. When he did ask something, it was if I was alright, and I didn't answer him for a while. There wasn't an easy way to, was the thing. It was both a 'yes' and a 'no.'

"I don't know."

"Fair enough," he said and leaned over enough to press a kiss into my hair then against my cheek before resting his head on my shoulder. "Has she ever —"

"Talked to me like that before?" I finished. "No."

"I didn't think so," Scott said.

"I mean, there's got to be truth to the way she feels. Alcohol isn't known for making liars." My chest was tight, and it wasn't in a panic-attack way, but in a sad way. Regardless of whether Juliet had meant it or not, it had been really fucking painful to hear. I wasn't used to words hurting. I'd take sticks and stones over that shit any day. Hell, I could take an all-out beating since I was a toddler, but this…

"Lakyn," Scott muttered. "You have a right to feel the way you do too."

"I did try to kill myself though," I said with a laugh, even though it wasn't funny. "I tried to give up. I wouldn't be causing her this much pain if I wasn't here."

Scott sat up and took my face into both of his hands, drawing my full attention onto him. "Listen to me, Lakyn. Anything that's wrong with her right now is not your fault. Her mother dying wasn't your fault. Her issues are not on you, okay?"

"Okay," I whispered, even though I wasn't completely sure. Scott nodded, and kissed me. It was deep and so, *so good*. I lost myself in him, and for just a little while, there were no scars on my wrists, no bruises on my knuckles, no drunk girl inside with a broken heart.

For just a little while, there was only the feeling of Scott's mouth on mine, his hands in my hair, his warmth holding me together.

For just a little while, that was all that mattered.

9
"YOU WANT TO MAKE A PORN STAR JOKE, DON'T YOU?"

Juliet slept all through Sunday, which wasn't out of character, and I was thankful for not having to look at her. Mostly because I felt like shit. I'd been expecting it, the mood dump that would come after I used up so much emotional energy, but it still sucked.

There was a whirlwind in my head that reminded me Scott knew too much. That the information he had wasn't something I'd given over willingly. He would look at me differently, like he could see the pain that was long faded, like he would know the stories behind broken bones, hidden bruises, and 'childhood accidents.' I hated that.

I hated that I was making Uncle Ben's life more difficult than it had to be. I hated that Rick had to move back in to keep an eye on me. I hated that Juliet felt pushed out of her own family.

I hated myself.

I tilted my head as I started another thin line of red just under the crook of my elbow, and felt another tear slowly slide down my cheek. I was raw and torn open and nothing was okay. I wanted to crawl back into bed and forget everything. I wanted to not matter.

Scott texted me, for the third time. I didn't bother to open the message to see what it was. I couldn't figure out why he cared, I definitely wasn't worth it.

I missed him, though.

I missed him enough that my throat closed up and it was hard to breathe. My fingers shook around the blade they were holding as I moved it down for another cut. Slowly, the tightness in my chest faded away.

I wanted to be with Scott. I wanted his bright smiles and his warm arms. I wanted whatever stupid joke he'd come up with on the spot, and kisses pressed against my temple. I didn't want to be alone.

But he didn't deserve to be surrounded by my misery.

A tear dropped from my chin onto my arm, smearing red across my skin. I was starting to make a mess. It was time to clean up.

***

Juliet didn't talk to me Monday morning. She had dark circles under her eyes, a sloppy braid, and looked like getting into her uniform had been a serious struggle. Rick watched her closely while we ate breakfast, but didn't comment.

I ate twice my usual amount, despite the fact that I wasn't that hungry, because I had no intention of being around during lunch. My plan was to go to the library and hide behind the back shelves until the full thirty minutes were up. I knew it would bother Scott, but I didn't want to talk about it.

I was avoiding, I was well aware, but it was a skill I was very good at.

I got through the day by keeping my head down and getting my shit done. I was purposefully late to my classes with Scott and early to my ones without him.

Matt caught my eye at some point in the afternoon and gave me a concerned look, but I simply shrugged and hoped he took that to mean I was fine.

When the final bell rang and I made it out, Uncle Ben was there to pick me up.

I was mildly confused, but took the solace of his truck over the idea that Scott might manage to catch up to me. "Hey kid," he greeted, ruffling my hair after I closed the door. "Do you think you can handle an appointment this afternoon?"

Seeing another head-shrinker was not on my list of things I wanted to do. I was tired, both emotionally and physically, and all I really wanted was to go lie down in the studio with Juliet and light one up. Too bad she wasn't speaking to me.

"Yeah," I said.

I dug my phone out of my pocket to let Juliet know where I was, so she wouldn't be stuck waiting on me. It was better that way really, I didn't think I could handle another ride in awkward silence. Then I opened the texts from Scott. There were seven. Two were memes, four were random thoughts he'd had during the day, and one was from lunch, asking if I was okay. He was trying to be normal.

That only made it worse.

The drive to the psychology office was short and silent, and the building itself had a different tone to it than I was used to. It felt like walking into a bank. Everything was shiny in a way that spoke of money, and I was glad I was still in my uniform instead of a hoodie and ratty converse.

"I'm not sure this will work," Uncle Ben admitted after he signed me in. "It's just a meeting, no pressure. But I think you're going to like her."

I hummed noncommittally, because in the line of therapists I'd seen already, I hadn't liked any of them. We sat down and I tried my hardest not to fidget. Normally there was a TV on, or games to play with, but this one only had a few magazines. My fingers were itching toward an old issue of TIME when voices from the stairs caught my attention.

The woman walking out was probably my uncle's age, petite but she held herself like she wasn't, with dark brown skin and pin-straight black hair. She was holding a clipboard in her arms and smiling kindly at the other woman who must have been her patient. I assumed mostly because she was crying.

The two split, the therapist checked her board, then she glanced around the room until her gaze landed on me. Her smile was inviting.

I didn't like her already.

Her shoes clicked on the tiles as she crossed the room, and I was grateful when she didn't hold a hand out for me to shake. "You must be Lakyn James."

I glanced at my uncle, and he nodded once before saying, "This is Dr. Anna Hoar. She's an adult psychologist by trade, but when I explained your situation she said she'd be willing to give you two a try."

I arched an eyebrow slowly as I turned back to the woman. "Dr. Hoar?"

The corners of her mouth turned into what was more of a smirk than a smile. "You want to make a porn star joke, don't you?"

"Only a little," I admitted.

My uncle heaved a sigh. "Lakyn, did you hear what I *just* —"

"Adult psychologist," I interrupted, playing heavily on the double meaning. "I heard you. You pulled some strings."

It wasn't a question so much as an accusation, but he still answered, "She's a friend of a friend."

"My wife thinks she deserves a new car every few months and your uncle generously talks her down when she shows up at his dealership," Dr. Hoar explained. "Well, usually. He does like to make money, after all."

I tried my hardest not to smile. "You're fucking with me."

"I am not," she said, making a cross motion over her heart. "Last time I was there myself he asked if I had any advice on teenagers with adult problems. I said I'd see what I could do. Shall we, then?"

I looked to my uncle one more time, he nodded, and I pushed myself out of my seat to follow her upstairs. I'd been expecting an office, with a desk and some sort of uncomfortable chair, but Dr. Hoar's room wasn't anything like that.

The lights were dim, the air smelled like apples and cinnamon, and it was warm. The carpet was plush and there were two large couches, with blankets thrown over the back of them.

"Would you like something to drink?" Dr. Hoar asked as she slipped her shoes off by one of the couches, and then crossed the room to a mini fridge. "Tea, soda, water? I'd offer you wine but you're a minor."

"I won't tell if you won't."

She shot me a grin over her shoulder.

"Tea," I said, feeling a smile quirk at my lips. I settled down onto the couch and she brought me a mug of hot tea before sitting on the other one. She tucked her feet up under herself, and I eyed her warily as I let the mug warm my hands.

I wasn't cold, but it was anchoring.

The tea was good, but the room was quiet.

"Benjamin warned me that you aren't very good at this therapy thing," she finally said. "Apparently you bump heads with adults."

I shrugged. "I think a lot of adults just don't remember what it feels like to be a teenager, and they fail in knowing how to handle us."

"Insightful," she decided. "And I'm also fairly certain, true. So, what is it that bothers you the most about being here?"

My gut reaction was not to answer, or to talk around the question, but I shoved it down. My uncle was treating me like an adult, believing that I could act like one, and I knew I needed this. I wasn't ignorant about that, I saw my own scars every morning. And if I couldn't do it for myself, then I could do it for Juliet. She needed me to be better, or at the very least stable.

"You don't know me," I said. "You don't know my story. What makes you think you can fix me?"

"I can't," she answered with a sly smile. "Only you can fix you. I'm just here to hand you the tools to make it easier."

I hummed and took a sip of my tea. She wasn't wrong, and I had no intention of arguing with her. "What else did my uncle tell you?"

"Why? Is there something you didn't want him to talk about? Or something that, perhaps, you did?"

She was prying, but she was doing it in a way that actually made me want to answer her. Explain myself, protect myself. "Color me curious."

"He didn't say much else, just that you don't like to talk." When I gave the smallest nod, she asked, "Why is that?"

"I don't like people to know things about me."

She considered that. "You don't want someone to use your secrets against you?"

"No," I answered. "When people know your damage, it's the first thing they see. I'm no longer Lakyn, or a boy, or a teenager. I'm scars on my wrists, and the judgment that…" I trailed off, realizing that I was about to go on a rant. My hands tightened around my mug. "Fuck. You're good at this."

Dr. Hoar grinned. "I know." She sat her own tea on the coffee table and regarded me more seriously. "Do you want help, Lakyn?"

"I need it," I told her.

"Yes," she agreed. "But do you *want* it? Because you're not going to get it, if you don't want it."

I took a deep breath in through my nose and let it out against my tea. Yeah, I wanted to get better. I wanted to know what waking up and not hating myself felt like. I wanted to sleep through the night, I wanted to look my cousin in the eye, I wanted to have a conversation with Scott and not need to bleed after it. "Yes."

Dr. Hoar nodded, seemingly pleased with herself. "Well then, I think we'll work out just fine together."

***

I was fucking itchy by the time we made it back home, like someone had gotten their fingernails into my skin and started scraping. I didn't feel exposed, just more transparent than I was before. It wasn't necessarily a bad feeling, but it was an incredibly uncomfortable one.

"Who's here?" Uncle Ben asked as he pulled up in front of the house. He had to go back to the office for a while, so I was just jumping out, and I hadn't been paying attention while we drove. Too lost in my own thoughts, with my head resting against the window. I frowned when Scott's Jeep came into view.

"Fuck."

"Lakyn," my uncle sighed but I barely heard him as I grabbed my bag off the floorboard and jumped out of the truck. There was no way Scott didn't know I'd been avoiding him all day, and the fact that he was here now was just weird.

I only made it two steps into the living room before I drew up short, because Scott was sitting on the couch across from Juliet, who was on the floor and still looking sour, a collection of textbooks and notes scattered across the coffee table between them.

"Hey," Scott said. His face was open, all soft brown eyes and an empathetic expression, pencil still raised to write. Juliet glanced at me but quickly looked away.

I nodded to the cluttered table. "Class project?"

"Top secret," he answered, which meant it was for Government because he thought he was funny and overused that joke. "Um, but, since you're here, maybe I could take a break for a minute and we could talk?"

Nope. I spun around on my heels and headed toward the hallway. My bedroom door still didn't have a lock on it but I didn't care. I'd sit against the damn thing if I had to.

"Lakyn!" I heard Scott get up and quickened my pace, but the jerk came jogging around the corner and caught up to me before I managed to get away from him. I sighed, then took a deep breath and faced him. He looked nervous, now that he had my attention. "Did I, um, are we okay?"

I quirked an eyebrow.

"I just haven't heard from you much today. Which is fine but after Saturday—"

"I don't want to talk about Saturday," I interrupted. "And I don't really want to talk to you right now either, okay?" I knew we wouldn't be here if I hadn't avoided him so much. If I'd acted normal, Scott would have too, but I didn't want to play this game. I didn't have the energy to.

He opened his mouth but closed it again, like he couldn't find the words, before he took a step forward. I immediately took one back, and hurt flashed across his face before he held his hands up like he was surrendering.

"Let me go," I muttered.

"Just talk to me," Scott said instead. "Fucking hell Lakyn, it's just me."

"Oh my god." I threw my bag against the floor and ran both my hands through my hair. I could feel myself being irrational but I couldn't fucking stop it. Anxiety mixed with a healthy dose of self loathing was fueling every emotion. "Just fucking go, Scott. Just leave. Please."

Scott shook his head and that unbearable itching was back, and it was my fault. I'd called attention to the problem, dragged him right back into it. "Christ, Scott. Would you just — the sex can't be that good. So just let me call it off. Because this —" I gestured to myself "— isn't going to get any better. And eventually I'm just going to weigh you down and I don't want to be the reason you stop smiling like a fucking idiot, alright? So would you do yourself a favor and just — Leave. Me. Alone."

He got that look on his face again, the sad lost one he'd had the night of the party, when Juliet had dug into me. My stomach rolled and the need to vomit caused me to take a deep breath before I turned my back on him, reaching yet again for my bedroom door.

"Everyone has problems," Scott muttered, and when I didn't say anything back he rose his voice. It wasn't quite a yell, but it wasn't the type of tone to be ignored either. "Lakyn. Everyone has problems. Do you get that?"

I looked over my shoulder to where Scott was shoving his hands in his pockets, like he was physically restraining himself from something. "Your dad hit you and your mom's awful. Okay, at least once a day my dad talks about how faggots are ruining the country and should be thrown in jail with the other perverts. And my mom pinches my cheeks and tells me I'm going to give her the most beautiful grandchildren one day. And I know it's not the same. I know it's nothing compared to what you've been through, but I know what it feels like to hurt. I know what it feels like to have something inside of you that you're sick of. The only difference is I drown mine while you try to cut yours out."

My hand fell away from the doorknob slowly, because I'd never heard Scott admit that his life was anything but picture perfect, and ignorantly I'd always thought it was. I turned just as he leaned back against the wall, hands still in his pockets, jaw clenched. "I don't get to be myself unless there's vodka and the lights are out and no one will remember it in the morning. Except for when I'm with you. I'm not here to make your life harder, Lakyn. I'm here because you make my life a little better, and I'm willing to bet I do the same fucking thing for you."

I sighed softly and dropped my head against the door, staring at him from across the hallway. I wasn't sure how either of us got here. It wasn't supposed to be like this. He met my gaze and for a long time neither of us said anything.

"I got a new therapist today," I said, softly.

He nodded and crossed the room, and I was sure he was going to kiss me, but instead he just pressed his forehead to mine. "I'm going to go finish my project. I'll see you at lunch tomorrow?"

I nodded slowly. Scott stayed where he was, his gaze locked on mine, looking for something. Whatever it was, I guessed he found it, because he nodded again and stepped away.

I watched him go, and he glanced back at me one more time before turning the corner into the living room. Finally, I got inside my room, and didn't even bother with taking my shoes off before I collapsed on my bed.

I was exhausted, and I didn't want to do shit, but I knew if I just lay there I'd run myself down even worse and likely end up with a razor to my skin. With what little energy I had left, I managed to grab my remote. I was pretty sure one of the *Paranormal Activity* movies was still in the DVD player, and I was more than happy to check out for a few hours until I fell asleep.

10
I HAD HALF THE MIND TO THROW A FULL-BLOWN TANTRUM.

By the time October came around I was starting to get sick of Juliet not talking to me. The thing was that I really fucking missed her. With Juliet, I could just be myself. Whatever messed up, awful version of myself that was. I didn't get that luxury with anyone else.

So, the fact that she was barely acknowledging my existence was driving me up the damn wall. I broke Wednesday morning on the way to school, slamming my hands on the dashboard in front of me. "Fucking hell, are you ever going to talk to me again?"

Juliet's hands tightened on the wheel but she didn't so much as glance my way. I had half the mind to throw a full-blown tantrum — kick, scream, bang on stuff, just so that she would look at me. It was a ridiculously childish way to deal with my problems, so I just ran a frustrated hand through my hair and pouted toward the window instead.

It didn't last. "You realize I did nothing wrong, right? Would you rather I'd just left you there? Let you go home with fuckin' Stella Wilson and that dude to do god knows what? What are you even on, Jules? How many drugs are you taking?"

"Don't start preaching Hugs Not Drugs at me, Lakyn James," Juliet said between clenched teeth. She still wasn't looking at me, but it was something.

"There's a difference between smoking a little weed and completely fucking up your brain chemicals and you know it." I was beyond irritated, which didn't happen to me a lot. Usually I stayed pretty calm, or at least unbothered. But here I was with one of my favorite people, watching her come apart at the seams. It was killing me. "I'm sorry. Is that what you need me to say? I'm sorry that I moved into your life without a warning. I'm sorry that me and my problems are overshadowing yours. What the hell do you want me to do? Tell me and I'll do it!"

Juliet slammed on the brakes hard enough I shot out a hand to catch myself, then she turned on me. There were tears in her eyes even though she looked pissed, and her knuckles turned white from her death grip on the wheel. "You were going to leave me."

"Jules, you can't —" I started, then blinked when I realized what she'd said. "What?"

"You fucking took a razor blade to your wrists without any intention of ever coming back from it! You did that to me, Lakyn. Why? What the hell did I do to deserve you leaving me too?"

"You can't stop here," I tried again, shooting a nervous look over my shoulder.

Tears streaked down Juliet's face and she shook her head before banging her hands against the wheel. "Fuck you. Fuck you for the nightmares about what your funeral would look like. For making me wonder about a world without you. For seeing a black dress in a store window and thinking *'I could have worn that.'* Fuck you, fuck you, fuck you!"

"Jules." Cars were coming, we weren't moving, my heart was pounding like it was on overload. She was crying harder now and the van behind us was getting closer and closer. "Jules!"

The light turned yellow. The van honked loudly. Once, twice, again. More cars joined it.

"*Jules,*" I said again.

"Get out," she said, weirdly calm.

"What?"

"Get. Out. I'm serious. I'm done with dealing with you right now."

"Juliet—"

"Get out!"

"Fine!" I snapped. I got out of the stupid car, threw my bag over my shoulder, and slammed the door behind me. We were so close to the school it didn't matter anyway.

I jerked my phone out of my pocket while I stormed over to the sidewalk, pulling up my messages and sending one to Scott asking where he was. He replied quickly with *'the parking lot'* and I made my way there without a second thought.

Scott's Jeep was easy to spot, but also crowded. He was sitting on the hood of it with Matt, talking to a group of his friends that were gathered around, spinning a football between his hands. I gritted my teeth in annoyance and slid in between the Jeep and the truck it was parked next to, leaning back with my hands shoved in my pockets. Scott glanced at me curiously, but kept talking until the others decided they were going inside.

"Be there in a minute," he said, patting Matt's shoulder as he hopped down. Matt waved my way, but I just nodded at him. Scott finally gave me his attention. "What's up?"

"Skip with me," I said instead of answering. "I don't feel like school right now."

"And do what instead?" he asked, a smile tugging at the corners of his mouth, although whatever was showing on my face was keeping him from letting it through.

"Me," I offered.

Scott hummed and tilted his head like he was honestly fucking considering it. I scowled and made a move like I was going to walk off. He grabbed my arm before I went too far. "I'm kidding. My parents are home though."

"No one's at my place."

He nodded toward the Jeep and I shook him off so I could go around to climb into the passenger seat. He sent off a text, probably to Matt, tossed his football in the backseat, then got behind the wheel.

"Want to tell me what's wrong?" he asked as we got on the road.

I shook my head and sunk into the seat.

"Okay." Scott dropped his hand between us and I took it without prompting, tangling our fingers together and holding on tight. I knew I shouldn't use him this way: to feel better, to erase the expression that had been on Juliet's face when she'd looked at me like that. But he was a much less damaging alternative to any other option. And he didn't mind.

I wasn't sure if Juliet would actually go to class or not but I doubted she would go home. Rick and Uncle Ben were already at work, so the house was silent when we got there. I unlocked the front door but didn't bother with any lights as Scott and I made our way to my bedroom.

There still wasn't a lock on the door but I didn't care. I threw my bag across the room and got my stupid uniform jacket off before rounding on Scott. He was stepping out of his shoes and rocked back when I was suddenly on him, hands framing his face, mouth crashing against his.

He pressed into me with a quiet moan, fingers stumbling over the buttons of my shirt until he gave up and wrapped them tightly into the fabric to drag me closer. My head stopped spinning as the rest of the world faded away. This was what I had needed.

I tugged my damn shirt free of his hold and got it undone myself, our kiss turning messy while my focus was split, until I could push it over my shoulders and get it the fuck off. I shoved my hands down the back of Scott's khakis, getting a grip on his ass and pulling him against me. I gasped at the friction and he bit at my lip, walking us backward until my knees hit the bed and I crumbled onto it, dislodging our mouths.

"Shoes," he ordered through a harsh breath, lips red and swollen, before going for his own shirt. I watched him reveal each piece of skin like a fucking show, surging up to run my tongue against the flat planes of muscle, squeezing his ass just because I could. Scott let out a hiss and I jerked my hands free to work on getting his pants off instead. His fingers twisted in my hair while I pulled the zipper carefully over his tented boxer briefs, my breath fanning against his skin.

He made a low sound when my hand wrapped around his dick to draw him out and into my mouth instead. A hum escaped my throat at the weight of him on my tongue, the taste, the fill. I could stay there forever, that much I was sure of. I wanted to make him feel good. I wanted to make him forget about anything but me.

He let me have it for a moment, murmuring incoherently, his touch running through my hair, down the side of my face, under my jaw while I worked at him. Until it was too much and he was too close.

"Lakyn. Lakyn." He pulled me off gently, his thumb grazing over my bottom lip, his chocolate brown eyes gone dark. "What do you need?"

"*You*," I whispered, and instantly felt it in every nerve of my body. I needed him. I needed him to make it better.

He smiled and pressed a slow kiss to my forehead. "Then would you get your fucking shoes off?"

"Oh my god." I managed to get the laces out of the way while Scott kicked his pants aside before he went for mine. His mouth found my neck and my head fell back to give him more skin while he got the button and zip undone, then I lifted my hips to help him get them and my boxers off. "Lube."

"Nightstand?" he asked breathlessly, and at my nod he moved to go dig around in the drawer. He tossed a condom packet my way, and, with shaking fingers, I somehow got it open while he handled the lube. I moved over to him and rolled the latex into place. Scott let out a surprised moan and dropped a hand to my shoulder. "Little shit."

"Yeah. You gonna fuck me, or what?" I asked, amused, searching out a pillow to roll up under my hips.

"Bossy, too," he said, and my mouth stretched into a grin as I fell back against the bed. He coated his fingers generously and I motioned him closer, wrapping an arm loosely around his neck to pull him into a kiss. His teeth dragged at my bottom lip and his hand found its way between my thighs, knuckles dragging gently across my dick before dipping lower.

My body tensed at the first bit of pressure and I sighed before giving a gentle nod, forcing myself to relax. His mouth returned to mine, and the world unraveled at the seams, unimportant and drifting away. He was the center of the universe. My everything.

He pushed into me when the stretch was enough and my hands twisted in the sheets and in his hair, mouth falling open in a silent gasp. I felt him everywhere, on my skin, in my fucking soul. His hand touched my face, tracing along the side of my jaw. "Better?" he asked.

"Better," I whispered, and melted on the last letter. This wasn't what I was used to. It wasn't clawing desperation and want. This was slow, and perfect in a way that felt unreal. In a way that made me feel unreal. I had no idea where he stopped and I began and I didn't fucking care. I was lost in a world he had created, weak to whatever he wanted to do to me. I trusted him to take me apart like this. I trusted him to put me back together after.

"Fuck," I breathed out when his hand on my dick shocked everything back into stunning clarity. Scott chuckled, pressing his forehead to mine and matching his strokes with the roll of his hips. Until I was arching up, fingers digging into his shoulders, words tumbling out of my mouth that I couldn't make sense of.

The end washed over me in a wave of comforting heat, taking all of my restless energy, all of my worries, with it. I came back down on sweat-soaked sheets to loose muscles and Scott's face pressed into the side of my neck. My fingers ran through his hair and over his back, while I murmured encouragements into his ear until he finally let go with a relieved sigh. Something in my chest swelled, some feeling I rarely ever let myself acknowledge. It was good and pure and a sign that I was in deep. That this boy in my arms meant too fucking much.

I aggressively ignored it. I wouldn't let it ruin this moment.

We lay like that, like the only two people in the world, until the effects wore off and the idea of being under the blankets was too pleasing to ignore anymore.

Scott pulled me to the bathroom with soft kisses and murmured words so that we could clean up, and then we were right back in bed.

He let me cuddle up to his side and rest my head on his chest while his fingers drew absent patterns on my shoulders, occasionally stopping in their path to trace the scars there. I was almost asleep when he spoke.

"Want to tell me what happened yet?"

"Juliet kicked me out of the car."

"What the hell? Where?"

"Close to the school, it's fine." I moved enough that I could look at him. "I asked her if she was ever going to talk to me again and she just broke down. Stopped the damn car right before the red light on Raymond Street."

"Fuck," Scott muttered, his hand moving to push my hair off my forehead. "Are you okay?"

"I guess." I shifted my weight until I was more on Scott than beside him, folding an arm across his chest and resting my chin on it.

"I didn't know she still wasn't talking to you."

"Yeah," I said. "She's really mad at me."

"About the stupid party thing?" he asked.

I shrugged. "It goes deeper than that. She told me she was mad at me when I first got here but I guess I wasn't paying close enough attention. I don't know. I've been too wrapped up in my own shit I guess. At some point, I'm going to have to stop being so damn selfish."

Scott leaned up for another kiss and I met him for it. It was the short and sweet kind that didn't have to mean anything else. It was simple, and I liked it.

"Want to watch a movie?" he asked.

"Please," I said.

I fell asleep to *Dark Shadows*, nestled in his arms, and hated how easy it was. There were no nightmares, no fear tugging at the back of my mind warning me to stay awake. I felt safe, and warm, and slept better than I had in years. Scott woke me up around three, by pressing kisses to every part of me he could reach.

I blinked a few times and looked up at him, wondering when he'd gotten dressed. I didn't even remember him moving. "I gotta go," he said, running his fingers through my hair. "Can't miss practice. I made you a sandwich, you slept through lunch."

"How long have you been up?"

"Not long," he promised. "You good?"

I nodded and tugged him down for a goodbye kiss before he left, taking his bag and any sign that he'd been there at all with him. I got out of bed to pull on my boxers and switch the DVD that was playing.

Scott had made me a peanut butter and banana sandwich, and I felt like an idiot for thinking it was the best thing I'd ever eaten.

When I settled back against the headboard it hit me that I missed him already, and I wondered when Scott and I had started doing something other than just fucking. Because that morning had been different. That morning had *meant* something.

I wondered when exactly I'd fallen in love with him.

***

My realization about Scott came suddenly and was completely unwanted. I'd gone and done exactly what I'd been trying so hard to fucking avoid: gotten attached.

I'd known from day one Scott was a bad idea. What the hell had I been thinking? I was messing up so hard. Why didn't I know how to just hit the brakes?

Juliet sure knew how to, maybe I should ask her.

"You seem frustrated today," Dr. Hoar mentioned, and I shrugged without looking up. I'd been picking at the rubber on the bottom of my shoe for the last ten minutes. She didn't like it when I went quiet for too long, though sometimes she just watched me to see if she could guess what was going on in my head. It was a weird game.

The truth was that I had plenty I could talk about. Juliet, Scott, everything in between those two. From being ignored to falling in love, there were a lot of emotions. The problem was that I was slipping back into that place inside of myself that didn't want to deal. It was dangerous territory.

"What's bothering you?"

I didn't answer, mostly because I didn't like lying.

"Okay," she allowed, "is it a person then?"

I looked up sharply and she gave me a wide grin that was too darkly triumphant for what we were doing here. "Oh, alright. Is it, mmhh, Juliet?"

"No. Mary fucking Poppins," I deadpanned. "I told her she could shove her spoonful of sugar up her ass and she didn't think it was very funny."

She beamed, which annoyed me, and I scoffed as I returned to my mission to destroy my shoes.

"You're feisty today, too," she observed.

"I'm feisty every day," I said, working my nails up under the rubber to give it another tug. She nodded and scribbled something on the clipboard.

"The fuck are you writing anyway?"

"Does it bother you?" Dr. Hoar asked, although it sounded like she already had the answer. I clenched my jaw and she laid both arms purposefully over the pages.

"What are you writing?" I asked a little nicer, like maybe that would make a difference.

"I'm evaluating your body language in comparison to your tone and referencing that to your psychological state."

My fingers ripped free from the rubber in my shoes and I glared. "Fucking stop it."

Dr. Hoar chuckled softly and picked up the board, twisting it around so I could look at it. My name was written across the top page, followed by the phrases 'constantly tired of people's bullshit,' 'older than he seems,' 'suicidal — but working on it,' 'feisty as hell today.'

"You're kind of a dick, you know that?"

She grinned and flipped the board back around. "I know. But don't act like it doesn't work on you."

"Oh, so you're only a dick for me?"

"Yup," she answered. "Are you going to talk to me now?"

"I really don't like you."

"Ah, but the beauty in all of this is that you don't have to like me. You just have to talk to me."

I sighed and pulled my legs up to sit crisscross, dropping my hands in my lap so that I would leave my stupid shoes alone. "Do you think teenagers can fall in love?"

"Why?" She asked. "Do you think you're in love?"

"Who said we're talking about me?"

"Your uncle's checkbook," she pointed out.

"Touché," I muttered.

I expected her to grin, the way she always did when she got the upper hand on me, but her expression stayed serious. "You know love can't save you, right?"

"I don't expect it to." I struggled to get my thoughts together. "He's not a Band-Aid or a fix, he's something additional. He makes some things better, he makes some things worse. He's complicated. But he's not going anywhere. And anyway, I don't want to talk about him."

"Okay," Dr. Hoar relented, even though I'd brought him up. "Let's talk about someone else then. Benjamin tells me you have a pretty good friend. Do you want to talk about him?"

Sometimes the world thought it was fucking funny. "No. Why's Uncle Ben telling you about Scott anyway?"

"Scott," she repeated, and wrote that down. I curled my fists over my knee while she said, "He told me because I asked if you got out of the house any. Aside from school, of course. They're still giving you space?"

"For the most part," I answered. "They still pay too much attention to me but it's not as suffocating as it was. So yeah, I can go places now."

"Like places with Scott?" she guessed.

"Sure," I said. "Sometimes. But I told you I don't want to talk about him."

There was a pause, and her hand froze before she managed to write something down. She folded her hands over the board again and asked, "Why?"

I hadn't intentionally dropped that piece of information, so I didn't know what to say: That I was pretty sure I had fallen in love with him? But we weren't technically anything to each other? Barely friends, maybe? Fuck buddies, definitely.

I slid my fingers under my sleeve to trace the scar on my wrist, feeling my pulse idly. I knew I'd have to answer eventually, but that didn't make it any easier. I almost wished I still had the stitches so that I could pick at them.

"Because he's a good thing. And if I talk about him too much, if I put that sort of attention on him, I'll twist my thoughts all up and ruin it. I'll push him away. Again."

"Again?" she prompted.

I exhaled heavily through my nose and nodded. The truth was that I had already thought myself sick around the problem that was Scott White. I wasn't quite sure what I was going to do about it, but I'd undeniably worked myself up.

"Good things don't last long in my world."

"Because you overthink them?"

"Because life isn't fair," I countered. "The nice people die too early, and the sweet girls do drugs, and the quality guy's in the closet. Life is ugly and twisted and it chews up all the good things and spits them back out broken and covered in slime. Until they're too weak to keep going. Until everything falls apart."

She listened and processed whatever she thought I meant quietly, tapping her pen against the plastic part of her board. "You're dark sometimes."

"I know. It's a character flaw."

Dr. Hoar shook her head before she got off the couch. "Well, we're out of time. But I'll see you next week? Maybe then you'll tell me what's bothering you so much."

'Not likely' was the retort I wanted to give her, but I bit my tongue until I could rephrase it to, "I'll try."

"That's all I ask."

***

Juliet did something that pissed Uncle Ben off enough that he took her car privileges away. Rick had been taking the two of us to school. I liked that better because I could sit in the back instead of next to her, which made the fact that she wasn't talking to me a lot easier.

On the other hand though, it made Rick aware of her grudge. Juliet and I had always been close, but since that stupid party, things had been slowly getting worse and worse. It irritated me for more than one reason, but mostly because I really didn't want anyone else sticking their nose in our business.

Rick intercepted me on the way to my room one Friday afternoon. I'd known it was coming, but I still sighed and dropped my head back on my shoulders. "Oh my god, what do you want?"

"I want to know what's going on between you and my sister, dude," he said, folding his arms over his chest. "This isn't like you two."

"Why the fuck are you asking me?" I shot at him. "Why not ask her? Why does everyone assume I'm the cause of the problem?"

"I didn't say that," he pointed out. "I'm coming to you because, generally speaking, you're the easier one to talk to."

That was a good point, although I wasn't sure anyone but Rick would think that. If only because I was cagey as hell and avoided things. I wanted to avoid this, which really said a lot about how hard it was to get Juliet to talk. "I don't know man, she's going through some shit I guess."

"She's always going through some shit. She's a teenager with a dead mother and a suicidal best friend. You've got to give me something better than that."

Guilt rolled over me and I shook my head before pushing past him and toward the hallway. "I don't know. I'm not her keeper, Rick, *fuck*."

I had to walk by her room to get to mine, and I paused by the door, wondering if there was something I could do. *Should* do. She was stretched out across her bed, sketching something, and looked over at me. Her expression was unreadable as she got up and I almost thought she might meet me in the hall. But then she just slowly closed the door, and I listened to her walk away.

I sighed and went to my room, threw my bag down and kicked the door shut behind me. I ran my fingers under the edge of my bed until I found where my razor was taped, then sat down on the floor. I rolled the sleeve of my right arm up and stared at the collection of thin scars there, a permanent backdrop to the one that should have taken my life. I didn't want to add to them, but I felt heavy, sluggish, and as usual, not very pleased with the person I was.

I rolled my shoulders and lifted the blade to the middle of my forearm, hesitating before pressing the sharp end to my skin. I hissed between my teeth as it cut, because it hurt in a way it normally didn't, and the blood that bubbled up wasn't nearly as satisfying as it was supposed to be.

I felt sick, and somehow hated myself even more. What was supposed to bring me relief only made it worse, and in a hot surge of anger I threw the damn blade across the room, pulled my knees up and hugged them to my chest, and sat there like that for a while.

My arm stung, my heart hurt, but there was something different now, something I couldn't quite put my finger on. I didn't even know for sure that I could understand it.

Eventually, I managed to push myself up and slink away to the bathroom so I could wash my arm off and slap a Band-Aid over the cut. I changed into my pajamas, gathered up my homework, and went downstairs to work in the kitchen and eat some ice cream.

I texted Scott a meme of the ridiculously photogenic guy *'entering a straight bar, leaving a gay bar'* with the caption **'dat you?'**. He replied with three laughing emojis, and I ended up smiling.

The world really did suck.

But I was still in it.

And I could still find reasons to smile.

11
"NO HOMO."

The rain beating down on my skin was miserable and hurt worse than my damn razors. It was sharp, cold, and for some messed up reason, I was barefoot. The asphalt was unforgiving and brutal, and I was running harder than I liked to, each breath like a stab to my chest.

Loud, angry barking reached my ears and I shot a look over my shoulder at the big black dogs that were following me. Six sets of bloodied teeth and snapping jaws. I couldn't stop, couldn't slow down, they'd kill me for sure.

I twisted around the corner of a building too fast, my feet sliding through water and screaming at me in protest. I nearly fell over, but managed to catch myself. It slowed me down though, and I cursed as I kept going; the barking was only getting closer and closer.

A Jeep was in the parking lot. A blue one, a new model.

Scott.

With what felt like my last burst of energy, I pushed myself to run faster. The passenger door opened and I was *so clos*e. It was right there. I grabbed at it when I got there, my right foot hitting the slippery running board, ready to throw myself in. I was there. I was safe.

I looked up and froze so fast it felt like I was back in Juliet's car when she'd slammed on the brakes. Everything inside my body hit a damned brick wall, I stopped breathing, my heart stopped. Because it wasn't Scott behind the wheel; it was my father, with a charming, society-approved smile, relaxing like nothing in the world was wrong. My mother leaned forward from the backseat, permanent sneer on her face. "Junior, hurry the fuck up, you're letting the rain in."

The seconds ticked away in my mind, one after another with a distinguished *tick*, the ever-present barking in the background getting louder. I knew what would happen to me if I didn't get in.

I knew what would happen to me if I did.

I stepped back and shut the door. The force vibrated through my bones — a death sentence, perfectly clear now. The rain let up.

The first bite ripped through the back of my leg, and I opened my mouth to scream.

"Lakyn! Lakyn wake up! It's just a dream! Lakyn!"

I jerked harshly and blinked rapidly in Juliet's face. She was white as a ghost, blonde hair a messy halo around her head. She had both hands on my shoulders, nails digging in painfully, and at some point, I'd ended up on the floor. Outside lightning struck, momentarily brightening the room.

My heart was beating a mile a minute and it was hard to breathe, but it got easier as her fingers lifted to my hair, pushing it off my forehead. She looked so much like her mother that I was comforted enough to manage drawing air back into my lungs. "What happened?"

"Nightmare," she said. She brushed tears away from my cheeks I hadn't even noticed were falling. I leaned into her arms, pressing my face to her shoulder, and she held onto me while I waited for the tremors to stop.

"You're okay, you're okay. I've got you," Juliet whispered, over and over, until she was sniffling and I realized she was crying too.

"Jules —"

"I'm sorry, Lake," she muttered. "For everything. For the stupid, godawful, selfish shit I said at that party. I didn't mean any of it —"

"It's okay," I interrupted.

"It's not," she said, but she either didn't have the energy to keep talking or knew I wouldn't listen to her anyway.

I took a deep breath to steady myself and said, "It's not. But neither is the shit I've been pulling. So let's just admit that we're both terrible people, yeah?"

Juliet snorted, but she nodded, and we sat like that for a while, wrapped up in each other, the thunder rolling lowly in the background, until my legs hurt from the awkward position they were in and my weight was dragging her down. I sat up and knew it had to be late. I didn't even remember falling asleep.

"You good now?" she asked, in a way that let me know it was fine if I wasn't.

"No," I said honestly. "But you can go back to bed. I'm sorry I woke you up."

She put *Bram Stoker's Dracula* in the DVD player, watched me climb back into bed, ran her fingers through my hair one more time, then left me alone. I made it thirty minutes into the movie when I admitted to myself that I wasn't going back to sleep.

I picked up my phone but it took a while to work up the courage to call Scott. I didn't think he'd actually answer, but just before his voicemail picked up, he did.

"Hey," he muttered through a yawn.

"Hey," I said. "You busy?"

"Nope. Just sleeping. No big deal. Whatever."

I chuckled and got more comfortable in the pile of covers I'd wrapped myself up in. "You can go back to bed, just stay on the phone with me?"

Scott yawned, but said, "Yeah, okay."

I fell asleep to the sound of his soft breathing in my ear, and the rain didn't even bother me.

***

That morning was hard. Partly because when I woke up, I felt like I hadn't slept at all. I could hear Scott moving around on the other end of the line though, and I rubbed my eyes before I cleared my throat and said, "You still there?"

"Hey," he replied, sounding far away. The phone moved, something clicked, then he was a lot closer. "Yeah. I'm still here. You okay?"

I didn't really want to answer, but I didn't want to lie to him either. Scott understood that by my silence, and didn't press me. "Want a ride to school today?" he asked.

"Nah," I said as I sat up. "I think Juliet and I might be alright now? So I should be good."

"Cool." I knew he'd want the details later, but it wasn't like he was going to make me tell him everything in the short amount of time we had to get ready. I didn't want to get off the phone. I wanted him with me, I wanted his arms wrapped around me, I wanted to feel safe again. My emotions were frayed already and it wasn't even eight o'clock yet.

"I'll see you there?"

"Yeah," Scott said. "Talk later."

I hung up before I could do something stupid like tell him I loved him and dragged my ass across the hall to the bathroom. I looked as tired as I felt, but there was no getting around that.

I climbed into the shower with my razor blade tucked between my fingers, sitting down heavily against the tub and letting the warm water wash over me. I lifted the sharp edge to my shoulder and held it there. Remembering how much it hurt last time.

I hesitated, then slowly lowered my hands into my lap. I didn't want to bleed.

Somehow, I managed to get myself ready for school, though I threw my uniform together messily and didn't even look at my hair twice. I was running behind enough that I was late for breakfast, but Juliet had set out bagels for me. Blueberry with strawberry cream cheese.

"You absolute goddess," I muttered as I fell into the seat next to her, leaning into her arms and picking up one of the halves.

Across the table Rick's eyebrows were raised, and he looked between his sister and myself before saying, "You two are cool now?"

"Were we ever not?" Juliet asked, and I ignored both of them in favor of eating. Rick drove us to school, and she sat in the back with me so I could lay my head on her shoulder. I wouldn't nap, but just resting was nice. Rick didn't even complain about us making him a chauffeur.

I slid out of reality at some point. I remembered walking into my first class, but the details after that were fuzzy. It was all a blur of sounds and faces I couldn't make out, until suddenly I was standing in the lunch line. I couldn't recall going there, or asking for the food that was on my tray. I nodded at the lunch lady and went to get a soda from the vending machine before heading outside.

Disassociating that way always left me feeling like the world wasn't quite real. Like I was already living in a memory, or walking through a dream. I tried shaking it off as I crossed the doorway, tried breathing in the cool air so maybe it would wake my senses up. It didn't, not really.

I bumped fists with Matt before I sat down at my usual spot, balancing my food on my lap and picking up a decent looking chicken sandwich. "What are we talking about?" I asked, because even though I usually didn't care, I needed something to keep me anchored.

Scott sent me a confused look but it was Matt who answered with a simple, "Sex."

"Disgusting," Kaitlynn said, sounding like she'd been a part of the conversation for too long already.

"Hey now!" Matt defended. "It's biological. Everyone does it. We need to stop acting like we don't. I just wish we got some decent education around here, is all I'm saying."

"Not everyone," said some guy that I didn't know. He threw an arm around Scott's shoulders and grinned at him. "Isn't Scotty here still a virgin?"

It was said like a joke, but the usual *'ooohhh*'s went around the group. I was pretty sure everyone thought Scott actually had game, even if he'd never had a girlfriend to back it up. I knew the truth of his virginity though, and took a bite of my sandwich as I stared him down.

He glanced at me before digging his elbow into the guy's ribs. "What makes you think that?"

His friend fell over, rubbing at the sore spot, but not giving in yet. "When was the last time you went on a date, White?"

Scott didn't answer, but the skin around his ears went red. I was curious myself, but I decided to take pity on him. Stupid, loveable idiot. "Like you have to date someone to get a little action. I bet Scott's had at least a hand around his dick at some point in the last, oh, few days or so."

Mine. Five or six times. Once in the janitor's closet even, if anyone was keeping score. Scott shot me a look to shut up but I simply smiled at him. Matt, however, seemed far too interested in the idea, a grin stretching across his face like he knew something. "Well, bro?"

Scott shrugged. "I can neither confirm nor deny."

"Oho," I muttered. "Big words."

He shot me the finger and I smirked. "When and where?" The words were out of my mouth before I could stop them, and suddenly the real world snapped into focus around me, killing the last of the haze I was in. Fuck.

We were at school.

Scott was pale but his eyes went dark. He was thinking about it. We were playing in dangerous territory. "In your dreams, James," he said.

"Right," I tried to recover. "No homo."

Nope. That made it worse.

There was no saving the situation. Matt looked surprised, Kaitlynn was suddenly very invested in the grass, and everyone else was caught between shock and disgust.

I'd forgotten myself. I'd gotten too comfortable. I swallowed thickly and turned back to my food, and whoever in the group had been carrying on an extra conversation stopped now that everyone else was so silent.

"So. You really are then. Gay?" It was Kaitlynn that spoke first, nervously, and I felt sick over it. I owed her this after being so awful to her before. I took a deep breath and glanced up at Matt, like he could offer me some sort of sage advice. He shook his head slightly, but I couldn't tell if he wanted me to keep my mouth shut, or if he was just trying to say he was sorry.

Either way, it didn't matter. I'd dug myself into a hole, I had to figure out where to go from there. I had the option to laugh it off, shake my head and say no. It would be so easy, just to lie. But I knew in the long run it would hurt me more. Besides, it wasn't like a shit ton of people just below their grade weren't aware of the truth.

The entire situation was dumb.

"Yup," I said.

"Gross," I heard someone mutter, and the guy behind me jumped about a mile back. I was exasperated, but it wasn't like I'd really expected anything more. The atmosphere changed on a dime, and I finally just stood up.

Matt opened his mouth but I didn't give him time to speak. "It's fine. I'll just go. I wouldn't want to make anyone uncomfortable." I was sure my words were dripping sarcasm but I didn't really care.

I'd barely eaten but I tossed my food, stopped by my locker for my iPod, and headed for the library. I didn't expect Scott to follow me. In fact, I knew he wouldn't, but it still hurt when I got there and he wasn't anywhere behind me.

The back corner was filled with old yearbooks, so no one ever went there, and it'd been a trusty hiding place since the beginning of the year. So I sat down, popped my headphones in, and closed my eyes against the world.

I didn't intend to skip my afternoon classes, but I did. I fell back into that place where time didn't really seem to exist, and before I knew it, Juliet was leaning down in front of me, obviously worried. I sighed and turned my music off.

"You weren't in Art," she said. "Or French."

"I've been here," I muttered.

She offered me a hand, but I waved her off before pushing myself up. It took more effort than I was proud of.

"You okay?" she asked.

"Don't worry about it, I'm fine."

"Lakyn." Juliet let out a heavy breath. "I know what I said that night, but you have the right to not be okay, and you can tell me if you're not."

"I'm never okay," I pointed out. "We both know that. Whatever. It's not a big deal. Stop carrying my stress on your shoulders, it's not good for you."

She held her hands up in surrender and motioned for me to follow her out. I barely remembered leaving, or seeing Rick, or the drive home. Once we got there though, Juliet wrapped a hand around my wrist and tugged me outside to the studio.

I sighed in relief and felt better as soon as there was a joint between my fingers. Juliet opened the window then sat across from me. I took a long drag before I asked, "What's been going on with you lately anyway?"

"Nothing," she said, and I sent her a sharp look. She shrugged, and I thought about pressing, but I figured it wouldn't do me any good in the long run. She'd just decided to stop being mad at me, and I really didn't want to put her back there.

"What happened today?" Juliet asked.

"Homophobic bullshit," I said. "Bridgewood's favorite pastime. Nothing new."

"How's Scott?"

I shook my head and sunk down farther in my beanbag chair, directing my gaze out the window. I didn't know how Scott was. I hadn't seen him for the rest of the day, and my phone had been suspiciously silent. Just in case, I tugged it out of my pocket. There was a text from Matt, but it was just an eye-roll emoji. Nothing from Scott. "I don't know."

"Ominous," she said.

I dropped my head back to stare up at the ceiling, raising the joint to my lips again. I blew smoke out in unpracticed rings and sighed. "All I wanted to do today was be with him."

"Oh," Juliet muttered, understanding what I didn't say. "That's scary."

"I know. It wasn't supposed to happen either."

The small room was silent as we finished smoking, then I fell over and said, "We need snacks."

"No we don't," Juliet muttered.

"Yes," I whined, "we do!"

"Snacks are all the way in the kitchen!"

"We need them," I said.

She huffed, but got up, and I grinned as I scrambled to my feet and followed after her.

She ended up making some awful cracker, cheese and pickles sandwich thing but it was actually surprisingly good. "I've missed you," I said, licking my fingers clean. "Don't ever get that mad at me again."

"Yeah, well, don't ever try to leave me again," she replied, under her breath, as she focused on pouring chocolate syrup into our bag of popcorn. I smiled, even though it wasn't really funny, and asked, "Hey, you want to watch a movie?"

She nodded and I led the way upstairs, turning my phone off as I went. Scott wouldn't call, and even if he did, I wasn't sure I wanted to hear what he had to say. In the meantime, I had Juliet, and I loved her too.

12
HAPPY PILL.

There was a fight in the parking lot Friday morning and I was only slightly surprised to find Scott in the middle of it. I'd missed the first punch but I had a feeling he hadn't thrown it, if only because he wasn't much of a fighter. The boy puked rainbows and happiness; it was against his very nature.

"Let me guess," I said as I slid up to Matt, tightening my grip on my bag. "Queer bashing?"

He side-eyed me and Juliet before nodding, his arms folded tightly over his chest like he was trying his hardest not to intervene. "Carter started it. Spouting off shit about…" He looked at me again, and then shook his head like he didn't want to finish.

I didn't know Carter, but watching him now, he just looked like an asshole. "How Scott's probably a fag too, since he hangs out with me so much?" I guessed.

Matt lifted a shoulder in a shrug. "If it makes you feel any better, he insinuated we were in a threesome."

"Hot," Juliet said, and grinned when I shot her a look. "Seriously, how much game do these jerks think you have? Nabbing Scott and Matt?"

"Ridiculous," I agreed, wincing as the fighting pair of boys went down. They were going at it hard, and my body tensed with the need to jump in. I wasn't actually that good at fighting myself, but it was dumb that Scott was getting hit because of me.

I couldn't help him though. I'd told him that when we'd started this mess. He was on his own. I couldn't hold his hand through anything.

A teacher eventually showed, flanked by a couple of worried looking girls, and the chanting onlookers scattered like cockroaches. Scott and Carter got dragged apart, even though they were still yelling at each other. Viciously.

"What's going on here?" The teacher demanded and Carter pointed an angry finger in Scott's direction. "That pervert tried to grab my balls!"

"Are you kidding me?" Scott yelled back. His lip was bleeding and he was holding onto a spot against his ribs, but otherwise looked alright. The side of Carter's face was torn from where he'd probably hit the asphalt. Good job, Scotty.

Matt raised his hand slowly. "If I could, Mr. O, I'm pretty sure Jess got the whole thing on camera? And you can figure out exactly what happened from there."

Mr. O looked between both of the boys and sent them off in the direction of the office with strict words, motioning for the girl named Jess to follow. Carter stomped ahead of them angrily, while Scott wiped at the edge of his mouth and frowned down at the blood on his palm.

I was sure he wouldn't look up at me, but I waited for him to anyway. Just in case.

He didn't.

**

By Monday, Scott was avoiding me. He'd ended up with a couple days of lunch detention for fighting, but that wasn't too bad. I didn't really care, I didn't particularly want to eat with him anyway. When I didn't show, Matt made it a point to let me know I was still welcome, but I turned him down in favor of just eating alone.

By Wednesday, it was obvious Scott was fighting with his friends. His usual group during class was strained, his walks through the hallway quiet and oddly sparse. I tried my best not to watch him like a kicked puppy, but it was hard. Mostly because I was honestly worried about him. Matt caught my eye on occasion and looked annoyed, but I just shrugged. There was nothing either of us could do.

By Saturday, I missed him. The lack of shared looks in class, my phone completely silent without his constant thoughts blowing it up, his absent company during homework or video game sessions. Without having him tugging at me for my attention, my days felt a little off, like I'd stepped into some odd parallel dimension

I was giving him his space, even though I hated it, because I was pretty sure it was what he needed.

By the next Tuesday, Juliet decided I was too fucking sad to leave alone and started dragging me to lunch with her crew. I didn't really like her friends. They were all older and had attitudes like they hadn't been born with a silver spoon in their mouths. More importantly, I didn't particularly like the way *she* was around them. My Juliet had never really been one to talk shit about people or laugh at someone else's expense. She wasn't particularly good at it, either. She seemed uncomfortable in her own skin.

They didn't hate me, but they didn't like me. I wasn't sure if it was an age thing or just a side effect of my general apathy. They usually lit up around lunch time though, and I enjoyed just letting the contact high soothe my nerves. I ignored the little baggies of pills being handed around. Juliet had made it clear that was none of my business.

That weekend, she asked me to go out with them. My gut reaction was no, but her face twisted up in disappointment and she asked me, "Why not?" It wasn't like I had plans with Scott, or anyone else, and I knew all I would do otherwise was probably lie in bed, watch movies, and be depressed.

I got up and put some clothes on. I had fresh cuts on my shoulders that had nothing to do with Juliet or Scott, but a particularly rough session with Dr. Hoar, and a desire to get somewhere that I didn't feel so numb.

It was the first time that I'd been to a party not thrown by some Bridgewood brat and it was funny how much of a difference money made. The house was only one story, dark and dusty. There was a keg, and I was sure I'd get lung cancer just stepping inside.

I didn't care enough not to indulge in cheap beer though, and I even actually played a few games, maybe beer pong, but I didn't really know and didn't really care, before stumbling into the living room. Juliet passed me a pill and I held it between my fingers for a long time, debating.

"It makes you feel good," she said over the music, and when I gave her a dubious look she added, "Nothing like last time."

I knew better, I did, but I still swallowed it anyway. I was tired of dealing with my feelings and making good choices. For a while, I just wanted to forget.

Juliet was a party trick. Guys thought it was hot that she'd make out with their girlfriends. She kissed without care. Any girl that fell into her lap. Some laughed, some got so into it their boyfriends actually looked jealous. It was one of her friends that pointed out I was gay too. It was said with a laugh, like the punchline to some joke. I was stretched out across a questionably dirty couch, watching the ceiling fan. Someone had looped glow sticks around it and the spinning, neon colors were fascinating.

Juliet was right, I *did* feel good. I felt calm, sated, like nothing could ever hurt me again. It wouldn't last, and I knew it, but I refused to let that bother me. My name caught my attention and I turned my head to the others.

They were taking bets, ribbing at their friends, something about how no one was brave enough to kiss me. I'd never asked to become a source of their entertainment, but whatever, no one could ruin my good mood.

"I'm not cheap," I said, looking up at the fan again. "You wanna play dares, pay up."

No one did.

***

The days blurred into a mix of disassociation and not sleeping. I couldn't sleep. If I did drift off I woke up screaming. Usually at home, but once in Art during a movie. Juliet covered for me.

She kept a steady stream of pills pressed into my palms and I threw them back dry. For just a couple of hours a day I'd feel lighter, like my feet weren't quite touching the ground, like I could pass my hand through a flame and never feel the heat.

It got too easy to sneak out with her at night. It wasn't like I was sleeping anyway. We'd round the block and climb into someone's car and trade our pajamas for whatever outfits we'd thrown in her trunk the day before.

The parties got lost in a haze of beer and a lack of caring. There were guys I knew and names I'd forgotten, but I'd only ever make it to getting pants undone before I'd realize the hands on me weren't *Scott's*. And fuck Scott White anyway. I should be allowed to enjoy myself, I thought. But I couldn't anymore, when it wasn't him, and the nausea caused me to push whoever was on me away and stumble back out.

School was hard and I hated it. The lights were too bright and the teachers were too damn nosey and there were too many people. I just wanted to do my work without anyone bothering me.

I missed Scott and I missed Matt, but every time the latter tried to talk to me it was like the whole world reminded him *I* wasn't his best friend. *Scott* was. It was stupid, but I didn't blame him.

I'd just take another pill from Juliet and let everything be okay.

Homecoming showed up out of nowhere and surprised the hell out of me, so much so that I was one of the few kids that still wore their uniform on Casual Friday. I liked football, so it was a shame. I would have participated more if I'd been fucking present.

I nearly fell on the way to lunch on Friday from exhaustion I was sure, and I blinked warily at the ground that hadn't managed to catch me yet. It took a while before I realized Kaitlynn was holding onto me, her brows drawn together in concern. "You look awful."

"Thanks," I deadpanned.

She frowned, and when I finally noticed I wasn't actually falling anymore, I stood on my own. Kaitlynn was chewing her bottom lip nervously. "Have they been awful to you?"

"Yes," I answered, because once she said it I remembered with vicious clarity — the shoves into my locker, the homework I had suddenly go missing, the trips in the lunchroom. Fuck them, though. "It's nothing new. I'm fine."

"You don't look fine."

"Yeah, I know, I *'look awful'*." I was done with the conversation. I needed a joint and another happy pill.

"When was the last time you ate?"

"*Kaitlynn*," I stressed her name out like it was impossibly long and hard to say. She was grating on my nerves. "Why don't you ever know when to stop?"

She jerked back a little, like I'd hit her, then narrowed her eyes. "You're kind of an ass."

"Yeah, well, you are what you eat and whatnot." That went right over her head and I would have laughed about it had I not realized just how fucking cruel I was being. I ran a shaky hand through my hair and sighed. "Shit. I'm sorry. I haven't been sleeping and I'm stressed the fuck out. Why are you over here talking to me, anyway?"

Kaitlynn looked toward where Scott's usual group hung out. Matt was leaning against a tree and spinning a football between his fingers, his face passive and unbothered to anyone who didn't know how to read him better. I did know how. I could see he was irritated by Scott. Who had his arm around a girl's waist. A cheerleader, long hair pulled back into some sort of perfect something, glitter on her face. I arched an eyebrow. "The fuck is that?"

"Claire Yates," Kaitlynn answered, her nose turning up at the name. "She's uh, not very nice. She's been latched to Scott's for a week now. I think maybe he's paying her off to get his straight guy status back. Or one of his friends is. Not sure."

I didn't recognize her, but that didn't mean much. Even with AP classes there were only a handful of sophomores I actually interacted with. There was something about her I didn't like though. She was trying too hard for one, and she put that detached look I hated on Scott's face.

"He's gay, isn't he?" Kaitlynn asked suddenly.

"Yeah," I said, then nearly bit my tongue off with how fucking stupid and unkind that was. I looked away from Scott and blinked at her. "I mean, what?"

She smiled sadly, not taking my admittedly weak bait. "It's okay, I figured. It's why you told me he wasn't interested, right? You weren't being a jerk, you were being honest."

"Sometimes those go hand in hand with me."

She lifted a shoulder in a shrug. "And you two were...?"

"Nothing," I said. "At least, nothing I'd let him label."

"Ah," she said, then redirected, "Matt and I were going to go get pizza. Do you want to come?"

I shook my head and started backing away from her. "Nah, I have plans. Thanks though." She looked disappointed enough that it rubbed me the wrong way, but I felt better once I could turn my back on her, and Matt, and Scott and Claire.

Juliet handed me a pill when I made it to her. That was what I needed.

***

I went to Homecoming but only because Juliet promised they'd spike the punch.

I didn't remember any of it, except that I was pretty sure we won and that Claire looped Scott in for a kiss so publicly inappropriate the teachers separated them.

I threw up in a fake potted plant in front of the office and laughed for a solid minute over it before Juliet looped an arm around my neck and took me outside. No one was paying attention to the football field after hours, so we walked the track with shaky knees and toasted to stupid things. I felt like shit the next morning but beer and another little pill washed it all away.

Scott came over Saturday afternoon. Juliet was home, passed out, but no one else was. It wasn't hard to figure out what he wanted when he showed up. I leaned in the doorway and stared him down, hands in my pockets, unimpressed.

Fuck him.

Scott opened his mouth, closed it, then shot forward and kissed me so hard I felt it in my fucking toes.

He tasted like alcohol.

The noise that clawed its way out of my throat sounded like a growl as my fingers knotted in his hair and I dragged him to my room. His hands were impatient, pushing at my clothes, slamming us both into walls. He nearly tripped over his own shoes before I slammed the door shut.

We parted as our attention went to our pants, getting them undone and off in a hurry. I was pissed, but I also missed the damn jerk, and the look he was giving me was so needy it went straight to my dick.

I didn't have enough self-control to tell my heart no when he looked at me like that.

Scott ripped his shirt free over his head and fell onto the bed on his stomach, grabbing a pillow to rest his head on, and reaching frantically into the nightstand drawer to find a condom and lube. He tossed them both at me before getting comfortable.

I climbed up on the mattress behind him, ripping the condom open with a little too much force. A deep breath filled my lungs as I told myself to calm the fuck down and leaned over to press kisses between Scott's shoulder blades, down his spine, to the two dimples in his lower back.

Scott buried his face into the pillow and the realization finally struck that I was watching him break down. This was him losing it. This was him at the end of his line.

The anger fell away, leaving me cold and unsure. I knew I said his name but I barely heard it. I wasn't sure how he did, but he took a shuddering breath and tilted his head slightly to look back at me. "Please."

My heart jumped. This was a habit I'd been trying to avoid, using each other to feel better, and yet, here we were. I sighed as I sat up again, letting my fingers drift over the curve of his ass. I expected him to be tense, or pushy, but he wasn't. Now that he was here, he was completely relaxed.

It felt wrong, on some level, but also like something we both needed. Neither of us knew how to use our fucking words. This was what we had. This was how we communicated. This was *"I miss you"* and *"I'm hurting"* and *"can you make it stop, just for a little while?"*. It was a bad idea but I was already too far in.

I worked him open with gentle fingers while my mouth memorized the muscles in his back. On occasion, he twisted around for an awkward kiss and I gave it to him, no matter how odd the angle. I could do this for him. When I tugged his hips up, he went to his knees easily, let me slide in all the way before I dropped my hands down to his and twined our fingers together. He felt so fucking good around me it was unreal, and I wondered how the hell we ever made it without this. Without each other.

"Move," he muttered, and I did. With sure, deep strokes to give him what he'd come looking for. My forehead fell to the middle of his back and my eyes fluttered shut.

I disappeared in the feel of him, his warmth, his want, until his grip on my hands tightened and his body bowed. One of my hands shook free and moved under us to get a grip around his dick, pulling him slowly until he went tense and crashed. He crumpled against the bed with a broken sigh and I slipped out of him without minding.

I jerked myself to finish, ending much more gently than he had, and wiped my hand clean on the sheets before I fell next to him. His eyes were closed, his breathing evening out, and I pushed at the sweaty hair laying on his forehead.

I thought about asking if he was okay, but we both knew he wasn't. Things had been too damn hard lately. This was him trying to deal with that.

I drifted off without meaning to and woke only because I needed to piss. It was dark out but the clock claimed it wasn't late. No one was home yet, at least. I nudged Scott awake and into the bathroom for a shower that we took together. He let me touch him, let me wash his chest and kiss him, but didn't say a word. He was exhausted, but clear and focused. Sober, finally.

He dressed and before he left, I walked up behind him, wrapping my arms around his waist and pressing my face to the back of his neck. "Don't ever fucking drink and drive again," I muttered.

His hand fell to one of mine and gave it a squeeze. He didn't apologize, but it was close enough, then he walked away. Juliet caught my eye from her bedroom, the judgment clear on her face. Scott hurried past her but I didn't dare break her gaze. Once I was sure that he was out of the house, I shut the door on her.

When he was gone, I still smelled him on my sheets.

Without him, I woke up screaming.

Bad fucking idea.

School. Home. Nightmares. Repeat. I had vague flashes of Juliet smiling but it was never quite right, Uncle Ben looking worried and wiping at my tears in the middle of the night, assignments with A's splashed across them that I didn't remember doing. Pills and drinks and pills and drinks and oh — *I was spiraling.*

I took too much, too fast, and the happiness crashed down and left me in a wave of misery. I wasn't even sure where I was, a bathroom somewhere, didn't matter though. There was a razor between my fingers and cuts on my forearm.

I hated myself. *I hated myself, hated myself, hated myself.*

The cut went too deep and it wouldn't kill me but it would bleed and bleed and *bleed*. I laughed as I kicked the door open and went to find Juliet because I'd promised, hadn't I?

What was the promise though?

That I'd try again, or that I wouldn't?

***

At some point in my life I'd become intimately familiar with hospitals. With the words *'self-harmer,' 'not an accident,' 'should we call family services?'* being thrown around the room like I wasn't there.

I was severely dehydrated, chock full of alcohol and drugs, and sleep deprived. I got an IV stuck in a vein it took them forever to find and stitches in my arms. All with a handful of questions that weren't important these days.

Sobering up was a bitch and a half.

I rubbed my hands clumsily over my face and blinked slowly to get used to the bright lighting. The room faded in and out but eventually my uncle's form came into view; everything was so *fucking white*. Matt had taken me to the hospital. I vaguely remembered Juliet passing me to him, claiming that she was too fucking high to help. I'd promised him it wasn't because of Scott in the car.

That this had been bound to happen eventually.

I didn't know where he was now. Or when my uncle had gotten here.

I picked at my hospital bracelet.

It said Lakyn James.

Uncle Ben was leaning on the wall with his hands tucked in his pockets. He looked like he couldn't figure out rather to cry or yell at me, and I honestly wouldn't blame him for either reaction.

"Hi," I muttered, just to break the silence, just to get it fucking over with. But I wasn't naive enough to think this little stint wouldn't follow me home. I blinked back the harsh reality of tears and tilted my head toward the ceiling. I'd just gotten some fucking freedom, and now I was back at the start. Didn't pass Go, didn't collect two hundred dollars.

"I don't even know where to start with you," he said. "The cutting. The drugs. Fuck, Lakyn."

I winced, because while Juliet, Rick and I had mouths like sailors, Uncle Ben didn't actually curse that much. At least not like that. Our vocabulary had come from Aunt Lily — while her husband had maintained that 'bad words' were only used for special moments, she'd put them in her sentences for no reason at all.

He sighed, and he sounded defeated, disappointed, both of which were so much worse than me just being in trouble and getting yelled at. "You could at least look at me."

"No," I said. "I don't think I can."

The silence stretched out and that wasn't any better. Yelling I knew how to deal with. He should hit the wall or curse some more or be like my damn father.

Instead he was my uncle, and he was a good man, and he cared about me. And I'd fucked up.

"I thought we were doing better," he said, and I could hear him pacing but I still wasn't going to look at him. I tilted my chin up higher to continue to avoid his gaze. He said, "I thought *you* were doing better."

"I was," I replied. "Until I wasn't. It happens sometimes. I'm not just going to be healed overnight. I warned you. Sixteen years of issues. A couple of months of therapy doesn't just make that go away. Not to mention being a teenager is kind of shitty on its own."

Quiet, again, until he settled heavily into a chair. "I don't know what to do here, Lakyn. I don't. Do I punish you? Do I put you back on suicide watch —"

"Please don't," my voice cracked like a traitorous bitch but I couldn't even *think* about being smothered like that again. It was too much and I would suffocate.

"I don't know how to trust you," Uncle Ben said. "And I'm not sure if it matters. What's the goal here? For you to stay alive, is that it?"

"There's a difference between being alive and living," I offered, swallowing thickly, because I wasn't sure if my point would get across. I'd been *'alive'* for years, but it'd never been worth it. It'd never been *'living.'*

Until now. But things were falling apart and I didn't know how to deal with that.

"When did you start doing drugs?"

I weighed the answer in my head. I didn't even know the name of what I'd been taking. I didn't remember the date when I started. Was it still October? "Ask Juliet. She gave them to me."

It was an awful, awful thing to say, but it'd been resting on the back of my tongue forever, just begging to get out. Someone needed to bring Juliet's problem to light, and now that my own secrets were stitched up, I didn't have anything to stop me.

"Damn it, Lakyn!" My uncle snapped, surprising me. "Don't drag her into this. The last thing I need is for you to lie to me too."

"I'm not!" I said, stressed, my heart rate climbing. I was going to cry and I knew it, and I really didn't fucking want to. "I'm not a liar!"

"You are when you're trying to protect yourself."

The words hit like a blow to my chest and my hands curled into fists. He was right, and I couldn't argue with that, and somehow I had managed to screw up something else. I heard him start pacing again. Finally, he gave another heavy sigh and said, "Get up, let's go home."

I waited until I heard the soft click of the door and then I just let go. The sobs raked out of me uninhibited and I gasped with how much it hurt to cry like that. I rolled over on my side and buried my face in my palms and just fucking broke until I couldn't anymore.

Then I got off the bed, dried my eyes, took a deep breath, and followed my uncle out.

13
"I NEED BETTER COPING MECHANISMS."

"I need better coping mechanisms."

"Yes," Dr. Hoar said soothingly. "I agree."

I pressed my forehead to the cool glass of her office window, gazing down at the cars driving past outside. It was funny to me how everyone else in the world had a life. They were all worried about something, going somewhere, with no idea who I was or what was happening. It was like being part of a funeral procession and watching normal people go about their day without realizing someone in the world was missing. I didn't like it very much.

"How are things at home?"

"Tense," I answered. The leaves had changed colors at some point. I hadn't noticed. It was almost Halloween, I hadn't made any plans. It was my favorite holiday. I should have been more excited.

"And Juliet?"

I wasn't sure if my uncle believed what I'd said about her or not. I wouldn't blame him if he didn't, I wouldn't even blame him if he didn't want to see it. Usually, she seemed fine. The only reason I knew what shape she was in was from being around her all the time. And from asking her to share her vices.

After the hospital, she'd apologized about six times, but I'd finally waved her off. It wasn't her fault. Sure, she might have been supplying, but I had made the decision to indulge. That was on me.

Dr. Hoar said that it was very mature of me not to blame my problems on someone else. I supposed if my fucking parents taught me anything, it was how to acknowledge my shortcomings.

"Do you ever feel like you're not sure what your place in the world is?" I asked, curling my fingers against the glass, still watching all the people down there that seemed to have a purpose. "I was supposed to be dead by now, ya know? So it's like: my road ended and by mistake I'm still here, but no one was prepared for that. So now I don't have any direction. The asphalts gone and it's all just unpaved dirt."

"Are you religious?" she asked.

"Sure." My parents had been awful about religion. They were the kind that only went to church because they knew it would make them look good. But Aunt Lily had loved church. We'd gone to a good one when we were kids. "Sometimes. I don't know. I relied on the idea of God a lot as a kid to survive. Now I wonder why he didn't help me sooner. But what's that story? Something about the man who gets stranded in the ocean, and asks God for help, but then turns away everyone who shows up with a boat? I guess this is my boat, huh? My uncle and you and this second chance."

"Maybe so," she said. I finally turned away from the window and went back to the couch, sitting with my legs curled up under me. I was tired, would have given anything to sleep right then. She was watching me closely, but I tried not to let it make me uncomfortable.

"What did you and my uncle talk about?" The first few days after the hospital he'd let me skip school and mostly left me alone while I detoxed. It hadn't been a pleasant time. It felt like having the flu and a fucking emotional dump at the same time, but important conversations had been paused in favor of taking care of me.

When I was better though, he made it clear that things were going to change. I obviously needed more help than I was getting. I'd started by handing over all the razor blades I had. I didn't want to be that person any more than he wanted me to be. I *wanted* to be better.

The next thing he'd asked of me was permission to talk to Dr. Hoar, about me, alone. It'd gone against every instinct I had and I'd curled my fists so tightly my nails broke skin, but I'd said yes. It was clear I had to. If I'd said no, I was sure the next resort would be back on suicide watch. Which was the last thing I wanted.

She considered me for a long moment like she wasn't sure how much information she wanted to give me. Then she said, "A few things. You, mostly, but I'm sure you know that." When I nodded she continued with, "He's not sure what the next step is. He's considering in-patient treatment."

"Fuck," I breathed out, dropping my head against the edge of the couch behind me. I willed the desire to cry down. In-patient would be worse than suicide watch. At least on watch I was at home.

"I told him I thought it was a little much," she said. "At least as far as I'm aware, you don't have an alcohol addiction, and the drugs are new. How were the withdrawals?"

I let out a slow breath. "Not bad. Then again, I was warned about anxiety, decreased appetite, and sleeplessness, all which I had before. I miss them, the pills, that high happy feeling, but it's fine. It'll fade."

"And you?" she asked. "Are you fine?"

I gave myself some time to think. "I don't know. Present issues aside, I have every reason to be happy. I'm just not."

She nodded. "How are your grades? I know staying ahead was important to you."

I rolled my eyes. "Even AP classes I can pass high and sleep deprived. School isn't hard."

She accepted that without comment and my session was up. Dr. Hoar gathered her notes then waited for me to walk out with her. "About your coping mechanisms. I think you need a hobby. Something that will distract you. Something that you can work on. Every time you feel like you need to cut, or take a pill, or drink — go do that instead."

"Yeah?" I asked. "What kind of hobby?"

"I'm not sure. Only you can figure that out. But try a few things, see what it gets you."

"Okay." I said goodbye to her before I let Rick drive me home, and the ride back was just as quiet as the ride there had been. I knew there was something on his mind, but I was raw from all the talking I'd already done, I didn't particularly want to drag it out of him.

Turned out I didn't have to, because he pulled into some parking lot about halfway there, drummed his hands on the wheel for a minute, then glanced at me. "Juliet isn't okay, is she?"

I sighed, but shook my head. "She's struggling, Rick. She misses her mom. She misses her dad too, which is my fault."

"How bad is it?"

"Not too bad, not yet, but it could be. I don't think Uncle Ben believes me."

"I don't think he knows what he's doing," Rick admitted. "He's trying, but he never expected to be a single parent of a couple of —"

"Damaged teenagers?" I interrupted. Rick shot me a sad look, but he nodded, and I understood. I really did, which was part of what made everything so hard. "I know. We're trying. We just need some help."

He nodded, then drove the rest of the way in silence.

After dinner that night, Uncle Ben held me back when the other two went to their rooms, and I picked at the fraying edge of my sleeve while I waited for him to tell me I was going away for a few months or something equally as horrible,

"How are you feeling?" he asked instead.

"Honestly?"

"Preferably."

I took a deep breath and placed my hands on the table to keep from ruining my shirt any farther. My stomach was all twisted up and I just wanted to go back to the way things had been before. "Shitty. Tired. Sad. Numb. Weak."

I saw him nod out of the corner of my eye, then I finally sat back and gave him my attention. I could handle this. As uncomfortable as I was, as much as I didn't want to, I could.

"So," he said, "I talked to Dr. Hoar. And last night I talked to Rick and Jules, and this morning I talked to your friends Matt and Scott, over the phone."

I swallowed thickly at the sound of Scott's name and hated how it tasted like a lie. I'd barely seen Scott all month, we were hardly even friends at this point, but he meant so fucking much to me. And my uncle had no idea. "About me?"

He nodded. "Everyone seems in agreement that you were fine until you weren't. That the drugs and the heavy drinking were new. Dr. Hoar says you've been doing good to push yourself to talk about things. Somewhere, something just went wrong. You got overwhelmed."

I nodded myself, it was pretty much true.

My uncle continued with, "I was seriously considering admitting you into inpatient care, but with what I know now it feels a little extreme. That could change though, if this keeps up. I just want you to be healthy, Lakyn. But to do that you have got to figure out how to handle your emotions. So, no more hurting yourself, no more drugs, no more alcohol, no more parties. Understand?"

"Yes sir," I muttered, which was polite and respectful but made both of us wince. My father had always been a 'yes sir' type of man, and apparently we were both remembering that.

Uncle Ben got up and switched chairs until he was sitting next to me. "I'm trusting you here, kid. One more time. Please don't make me regret that, okay?"

"Okay," I said.

"Anything else you want to talk about?"

There was still Juliet, but I no longer knew how to bring her up without him thinking I was avoiding things. I'd put that problem in Rick's hands, that was going to have to be enough. And of course, there was Scott, but was there really? Scott was nothing but a *'what could have been'* these days.

"No."

Uncle Ben nodded. "Something's bothering you, you tell me. You want to go somewhere, you ask. You need to talk to someone, you do it. It doesn't have to be me, just talk to *someone*. I'm not going to cage you in but I can't not know how you're doing anymore."

"Okay," I said again. Then he pulled me into a headlock and I laughed for the first time in a while, fighting him off with very little seriousness until he finally gave in and told me I could go. I went up to my room knowing I wasn't going to sleep well, but at least I was home.

***

Scott was sitting on the hood of his Jeep before class on Monday morning without his usual crowd, and caught my eye when I went to walk by. I hesitated, and Juliet stopped next to me, but I eventually waved her off and went to stand in front of him.

"Hey," he said.

"Hey," I repeated.

Scott looked down at his lap and tapped his fingers against the dark blue metal of the hood. "Heard you were in the hospital over the weekend. You okay?"

"Few stitches, no big deal."

He nodded a couple of times and rubbed awkwardly at the back of his neck. It was rare to see him like this — unsure, unhappy. I didn't like the tension set in his shoulders, but it wasn't like I was allowed to rub it out either. Just before I was about to take a step back, he spoke again, "I'm sorry. For the way I've been acting. I didn't know —"

"I shouldn't have said what I said," I interrupted. "That day at lunch. Joke or not. I'd forgotten where I was and —"

"And I should have taken your side," Scott said, looking up at me again. "I know that. I know I've been a shitty friend lately. I just, with the way everyone reacted..."

"You panicked." I shrugged. "I know what it feels like, Scotty. Been there, done that. I get it. It's just another one of the reasons why we shouldn't have started what we did."

"Yeah, but, I didn't mean to end it either," he said. "At least, not like that. I shouldn't have been avoiding."

"We're avoiders, it's in our veins. Cuts or drinks, doesn't make much of a difference. The outcome is still the same. How much alcohol have you had in the last few weeks?"

"How many stitches did you have to get?" he shot back.

I smiled sadly. "A lot."

He nodded, because we both got our answer. Scott slid off the Jeep and picked his bag up off the ground. "I've had a hell of a time lately. I meant it, when I said you made my life easier. But there's a difference between my personal life and my school life and, well, both of them have been a lot fucking harder without you."

"I guess you're going to have to let them combine, then," I replied. "How's Claire?"

Scott winced, and I thought I'd feel good digging that knife into him, but I didn't. If anything, I felt worse. He looked at the school like it was the last place he wanted to be and shook his head. "Do you want to skip?"

"I can't. I'm being watched. I have study hall before lunch though, if you want to cut out early we can go grab something to eat?"

Scott nodded. "Yeah, okay. See you then."

***

School seemed longer when I was sober, and it felt like a year before I made it to study hall. I texted my uncle and let him know what I was doing, even though he hadn't asked for constant updates, but I figured if I gave a little I'd get a little.

Scott was in the courtyard talking to Claire when I got there, and something about the set of his back told me to keep my distance. He was doing that politely removed thing he did whenever he talked to girls. Engaged, with his body language clearly saying *no*. She either didn't know how to read that or didn't care, because she pressed her lips to his cheek, even when Scott leaned away.

I considered going back to the library and not dealing with any of *that*, but before I managed to actually move, Scott turned around and saw me. I lifted my chin in greeting and started off toward the parking lot. He met up with me, and I shot a look behind my shoulder just in time to catch Claire's glare as the warning bell for class rang.

"Wow. Thanks for that. I really needed more people to hate me."

Scott's mouth was set in a tense line and he sighed harshly through his nose. "She won't leave me alone."

I raised an eyebrow because Scott was notorious for being too damn nice to get his point across, which was why the incident with Kaitlynn had happened.

"Were you clear?"

"Yes," he answered. "I said the iconic *'I think we should just be friends'* line and everything. How much clearer could I have been?"

I shrugged and climbed into the passenger seat of the Jeep. We had about an hour and a half for lunch, and grabbed fast food burgers before Scott drove us just outside the city, where there was an old abandoned drive-in theater.

Technically, it was privately owned property, but no one seemed to mind when the teenagers used it to loiter. As long as they weren't burning shit. Given the time of the day it was empty, and Scott popped open the back hatch so we could sit there while we ate.

I let him settle between my legs with his back on my chest and ran my fingers through his hair while I worked on a chocolate milkshake, enjoying the cool fall weather. We hadn't talked about much, and while part of me felt like I shouldn't be there at all, another felt like it was the first time all month I'd been really comfortable.

"How did you do it?" Scott asked softly. Until then I'd almost thought he was asleep, he was relaxed enough to be, but now his brown eyes opened and looked up at me. "Deal with the backlash."

"Said 'fuck it' and moved about my business," I answered. "Then slit my wrists a couple of months later, so I'm not the best example."

Scott chuckled softly and shook his head. "Good point."

"I outed you to Kaitlynn."

There was a beat of silence, then he said, "I know. She told me. Promised she wouldn't tell anyone else, but that she figured I could use at least someone that knew the truth. Until I was ready to, ya know, tell everyone."

I wanted to ask him when he thought that would be, because I missed him, and I missed touching him. But it didn't feel fair. I knew it wasn't fair to me either, though. He was one more secret, and my current situation was making that weigh on me. Something was going to have to change.

But until then, I was going to indulge just a little.

***

Scott waited until two nights before Halloween to ask if I wanted to go out with him and Matt. I was walking to lunch with Juliet when it happened — trying to convince her to ditch her shit friends — and paused out of shock, over the question and the fact that he was talking to me in public again. He seemed stressed about it.

"Is Claire going?" I asked, but before he could answer Juliet had cut in with a quick, "Claire Yates?"

Scott winced and didn't answer my cousin. "No. But Kaitlynn might come, and Jules you're more than welcome to join. I'm sure she would like having another chick tag along."

"I can't party," I said.

He shrugged. "We're going trick-or-treating."

"You are not," I accused.

"Yes we fucking are," Scott said. "I even have a candy bucket for you to use."

I side-eyed him because I was pretty sure he was bullshitting me. "I'll ask my uncle."

He gave me one of his stupid bright grins, nodded, then left us alone Juliet did skip eating with her friends after all in order to fill me in on how much she did not like Claire Yates. Evidently my cousin had more classes with the girl than I did, and had some particularly nasty stories to share. It was weird to think that I hadn't been the only kid bullied in my family. Juliet was just better at hiding it.

Like me, Uncle Ben didn't seem convinced that trick-or-treating was actually how a few of the most popular kids in Bridgewood wanted to spend their Halloween, but a call to Matt's mother confirmed it was. He had a little cousin that he was the *Nino* to and always took her and a couple of friends out.

Juliet decided to go, which surprised me since she'd been planning on attending some shady-ass party. I expected her to use it as a cover up, but she went with me to throw together a last-minute costume. I just ended up with a pair of devil horns and let Jules put pointy acrylic nails on me. I painted them black, for the aesthetic.

It was a good night, spent on sugar rushes and laughing at the different responses we got from various adults. I made a game out of 'finding Waldo' since that was Scott's idea of a costume, and although he acted annoyed, I knew he liked it. If the quick handholds hidden by the shadows were anything to go by.

The fact that Uncle Ben had trusted me enough to let me go made me feel lighter. I'd still messed up, but it was nice to know it was only a bump in the road, not a full stop. Things were going to be okay.

It was even possible that *I* was going to be okay.

14
"WHY IS LIFE SO HARD?"

I tried my best to take Dr. Hoar's advice and find a hobby, but it seemed to be much easier said than done. The problem was that there weren't a lot of things I actually enjoyed doing. I liked video games, but not by myself. They had a tendency to make time disappear, and that felt too much like disassociating. I'd skateboarded back in middle school, but mostly as a cover for why I had so many bruises, so I'd never been *good* at it.

Sports were a no-go. I wasn't too into team playing, and while I liked being artistic it felt too much like work for me to really get into it for fun. I liked running, and I liked going to the gym, but it was really only on weekends that I could join Scott or Matt. They got the most of their workouts done at school, and it just wasn't the same by myself. I did run a couple of miles on occasion, listening to playlists Juliet put together for me, but it just wasn't *right*.

I liked doing Scott. But that was another one of those things I didn't always have access to.

He was also driving me crazy which didn't help matters at all. It was the fucking way he looked at me, the way he moved, the way he laughed. It was like the drugs had made me forget how much I loved him, and when sober I suddenly ached with need.

I was lying across the coffee table thinking about my life choices when Juliet walked in on me. She hesitated, then said, "Alright. I can't not ask. What the hell are you doing?"

"Wallowing, I think?" I answered, not bothering to sit up. My cheek was pressed into some sketchbook paper that had skulls hastily drawn on them. I had a feeling they'd imprint on my skin if I moved. Still wasn't cool enough to make me actually do it.

"Scott?"

"Isn't it always?" I heard more than saw her cross the room to sit down in front of me. She picked up my pencil and started doodling on a corner of the page that I wasn't lying on, and I sighed. "I'm supposed to be finding a hobby. It's not going well."

"You have interests," she said.

"Yeah, I know that. But I feel like a toddler who never learned how to play alone. It's like everything I want to do requires another person."

"You have interests other than sex."

"Ha ha." I sat up then, holding my fingers to the page to keep from taking it with me. When I pointed at my cheek Juliet nodded. So it did imprint. Cool, temporary tattoo. It probably looked badass.

She seemed good, but she'd been more sober herself since my latest hospital stint. I wasn't sure if it was because she felt guilty, or because Uncle Ben had listened to me enough to keep somewhat of an eye on her. Either way, we weren't talking about it. It was better for our relationship, in a completely unhealthy and selfish way.

"Mom used to draw, do you remember?" she asked.

"She wasn't very good at it."

Juliet smiled, but with an edge of sadness, and my heart felt heavy at the sight of it. We all missed Aunt Lily. I wondered how things would be different, if she was still around. Juliet wouldn't be on drugs, Uncle Ben wouldn't be so stressed, Rick would be out living his life.

"It was always funny to me, how good she was at making clothes from a sketch that looked *nothing* like what she was actually seeing," Juliet said. "I miss that. Making things with her."

"You should do it again. By yourself."

She scoffed. "Are you saying *I* need a hobby?"

"Couldn't hurt," I said carefully. She ruffled my hair and stood up, leaving me alone in the living room again. I glanced at the drawing she'd done. A smiley face, though if I tilted my head to the side it looked sad. Optical illusion bullshit, and another reminder that she needed just as much help as I did.

One day she would get it. I just hoped she wouldn't have to take the same path I had.

* * *

Scott was talking a mile a minute but I hadn't heard one word. I was distracted by the way he'd lick his lips between sentences, momentarily forgetting his place, then bouncing up on his toes when he remembered and launched in again.

It was adorable and I was so fucking gone it was ridiculous.

He'd met up with me on the way to lunch, rambled all through the line in the cafeteria, then followed me outside. The weather was cooling down with winter approaching, which meant a lot of people had migrated into the cafeteria, but I didn't mind the cold. Scott didn't either, apparently. I was pretty sure he was talking about a TV show. I didn't really care about the details, but I liked how excited he got over it. It pulled at my stupid heart.

"Anyway," he said, bright-ass smile still on his face. "What's going on with you?"

"Huh?" I asked, the change of topic shocking me enough that I tore my gaze from his mouth.

Like the smug bastard he was, Scott's smile turned into a smirk, like he knew that I hadn't been paying attention. "You're all fidgety, lately."

I frowned and took a bite of my food, shrugging my shoulders. "Dr. Hoar says I need to find a hobby. It's more difficult than I originally thought. She's such a dick sometimes."

Scott laughed over her name, we always did. It was fucking immature, but neither of us could help it. "You just don't like it when people get under your skin. And that's exactly what she's doing," he pointed out. "That's why you don't like her."

"How do you know?" It wasn't like I'd ever explicitly told Scott what Dr. Hoar and I talked about. He didn't even know why she'd said I needed a hobby.

Then again, I figured he could guess.

"Because you get all cagey and agitated like this when someone gets too close to you," he said. "I should know, you do it to me all the time."

I rolled my eyes. "Fuck you."

"When?" Scott asked, clearly amused. "Today? Right now?"

My heart jumped and I looked around to remind myself that we were, in fact, at *school*. But my little spot by the stairs gave us a semblance of privacy. I knew it wasn't to be trusted, but there really wasn't anyone else around.

This sort of stuff was also what had given us so many problems last time though. Five minutes of pleasure wasn't worth a lifetime of hell and all that bullshit. Scott's fucking grin was pure temptation though, and for some reason I always liked to damn myself.

I lifted a shoulder, smirking down at my food. "Maybe."

"You're awful," Scott decided. "Simply the worst."

"True," I said. "You like it."

"True," he repeated.

"I told you to leave me alone though," I pointed out. "You were the one who wouldn't listen. So what can you do now?"

"Buckle up and enjoy the ride?"

I grinned at him. "Are you going to be doing the riding then?"

Scott licked his lips slowly. "Do you want me to?"

"Maybe," I said again.

He opened his mouth to say something else but the sound of heels on the stairs stopped him. A girl came around the corner and sighed out of exaggerated relief. "Scott! Cupcake, there you are!"

I'd never actually seen Claire Yates up close, but at first glance she was model pretty. Perfect in a way most teenagers never were. At second glance though, there was just something *off* about her.

When Juliet had been a child she couldn't go anywhere without people telling her how gorgeous she was. Aunt Lily had always said it was fine, but that beauty was deeper than just the skin, and a nice personality could make an attractive person. Looking at Claire, I thought the opposite was also true. Her skin was pretty, but something about her wasn't. It was horribly judgmental of me, but she was making me uncomfortable in a way I couldn't quite explain.

She bent down and easily picked up the tray from Scott's lap, wrinkling her nose at it. She had two friends behind her, both typing away on their cellphones, and I ignored them in favor of watching Scott, who had suddenly tensed.

"What's up, Claire?" he asked warily.

"It's Wednesday," she answered. "Remember we agreed that you would take me to lunch on Wednesdays? It's a tradition, all of our boyfriends do it, right girls?"

The two behind her nodded without looking up, and Scott's jaw clenched. I rested a hand on his knee to calm him down, and Claire's sharp gaze jerked over to me as if she'd just realized I was there.

Her lips pursed. I snatched my hand back.

Scott shifted nervously and said, "I thought we talked about this?"

She blinked, all mock innocence. "About what, Cupcake?"

That was really fucking annoying. He glanced at me, I shrugged, and he sighed before pushing himself to his feet. "About us, just being, you know, friends?"

Her expression only got darker, like she hadn't been expecting that, and something in my stomach twisted in a really gross way. No, I didn't like her *at all*. I tilted my head back to watch the other students coming down the stairs, knowing Matt would be in there somewhere. It was Kaitlynn who saw me first, and tugged on Matt's sleeve to catch his attention. He was grinning, at least until he saw my face.

Scott and Claire were still talking but I'd missed some of it when I turned back to them. She'd dropped the tray, the girls behind her had stopped looking at their phones, and Scott was stuttering. Then she slapped him.

Hard.

I suddenly knew what that tight feeling in my stomach was as I watched Scott take a step back. The side of his face went red immediately and before I'd even managed to get up she was hitting him again. And again. He wouldn't hit her back, I knew he wouldn't, but when he caught her wrist her knee went into his stomach.

"Hey!" Matt shouted, coming over, always there to save our asses. The grip he got on Claire was stronger than Scott's had been, and he jerked her back like a ragdoll. She screamed, and even after he'd let her go, she continued to overstep and crumbled to her knees with a sob, cradling her wrist to her chest. He hadn't grabbed her that hard, he wouldn't.

Manipulative bitch.

We were gathering a crowd, Claire's friends were cooing over her, but Matt went right to Scott. The onlookers were confused in a way that clearly said they didn't know how to react. Had a girl really hit a guy? Had Matt Alvarez really pushed a girl?

"I'm fine," Scott was saying, doubled over and wincing slightly. Matt nodded, but didn't look like he actually believed him. He helped him up and Scott's hand stayed on his stomach, but he allowed himself to be passed to Kaitlynn. She directed him out of the crowd, working like a human shield.

Matt caught my eye and nodded after them. "Go. I'll clean up this mess."

I'd been frozen until then, anxiety creeping through my veins, but I pushed it down in favor of nodding and catching up with Kaitlynn. Everyone's attention was on Scott, the whispers already starting.

Kaitlynn took us to the diner she worked at part-time — a family owned place that didn't open for another few hours. She let Scott and I sit on the couches around the fireplace, brought him a ziplock baggie full of ice that he pressed into his stomach, and left to make sandwiches.

Scott settled down with his head in my lap, looking infinitely younger than I'd ever seen him. He'd been hit worse, we both knew that. Carter had made a bigger mess of him, and it wasn't like he didn't play football, but something about this was different. Misguided or not, Claire had believed he was her boyfriend, and she'd *hit him*.

I ran my fingers through his hair soothingly, and almost didn't hear him when he asked, "Why is life so hard?"

"I don't know," I answered sadly. "But I wish it wasn't."

***

By Thursday there were a handful of new rumors: Scott had hit Claire first, Claire had kicked his ass, Matt had actually been the one to hit her and Scott had jumped in to defend her honor, Claire had cheated on Scott with Matt or vice versa and that was what the fight was about, and the occasional rumor that Scott and I were still banging and Claire had found out.

That one was old news and rarer, but ironically closer to the truth.

Because adults were idiots, Matt and Scott both ended up with detention, and Claire had a brace on her arm even though Matt had barely grabbed her hard enough to bruise. No one quite believed that she had attacked first, but regardless, there was a rule put in place that she wasn't supposed to be anywhere near either boy. That was the only good thing to come out of it all. Matt was irritated, Kaitlynn was annoyed by the gender stereotyping, and I was just *done*.

By Friday, Scott was avoiding me again.

The thing was that I couldn't handle it anymore. The constant back and forth shift, the needing me and pushing me away, the secrets. The week dragged by painfully slow and each day it got harder.

I knew he was going through his own shit, that he had his own problems, but I was well aware that I made up some of those problems. I was either the reason or the cause or the instigator to most of them.

He wasn't hurting me on purpose, and I wasn't hurting him on purpose. But the fact of the matter was that jerking each other around was becoming toxic.

For both of us.

I gave it another week of silence before I broke down. It was too hard. I knew better than to go to Juliet for a ride, so I hit up Rick instead. I figured that if I asked him not to, he wouldn't pressure me for details. He'd hesitated, but taken me to Scott's anyway, waiting in the car without a word. The Whites weren't home, wouldn't be until eight or so, and Scott himself had just gotten out of practice.

He smiled when he saw me, but it was pulled tight, and his body was mostly blocking the doorway. It was a protective stance that hurt my stupid heart. I shuffled my feet, sighed, and asked, "Can I come in?"

"'Course," he said, and moved out of my way. "Want a drink?"

I shook my head and Scott's expression closed off even more, like he'd finally had to admit this wasn't the good kind of house call. I lowered myself onto the couch, pulling my legs with me. Dr. Hoar would have probably pointed it out as a defense mechanism. Scott likely didn't notice.

"What's going on, Lake?" he asked as he sat next to me. Maybe he did notice my posture for what it was after all, because he left a good bit of distance between us.

I took a deep breath and tried to look somewhere that wasn't at him, but none of the other options were any better. The floor was where we did homework, I'd sat in his lap and made out with him in the recliner, we watched a shit-ton of movies on that TV. Why was I here?

"I don't think we should do this anymore."

The words hung heavy between us and my heart lurched in a painful way. I could take them back, there was still time, but I bit at the inside of my cheek to keep from saying anything. Finally, I looked at Scott. His hair was wet and pushed back, his t-shirt sticking to still damp skin. I always loved the way he looked wet. There was a drop of water streaking from his jaw to his collarbone. I could hold him down and follow it with my tongue. Erase all of this.

"We're not doing anything, remember?" he said, but his voice was raw and the joke fell flat. "You made sure of that."

I tore my gaze away from him again. I wouldn't cry. I *wouldn't*. I stared straight at the fucking wall and said, "Then I don't think we should be friends anymore."

Silence. It felt like it stretched on for hours but I knew it couldn't have. I didn't look at him. My hands were shaking.

"Why?" His voice cracked and my heart broke.

"Because." I took a deep, shaky breath. "Because I'm tired of being your secret, Scott. It hurts too much. I'm tired of feeling empty when you're not around, I'm tired of knowing you'll make things better but I can't have you when I need you. I'm tired of having to shove my hands in my pockets so I don't reach for your hand at school. I'm tired of watching you fall apart, week after week, because of how you feel and what it means to you. And I know that me being so fucking tired is putting too much pressure you. It's all too hard. Harder than it's supposed to be."

"You want me to come out?" he asked, a little desperately. Like he thought that would fix everything. "Is that what this is about?"

"I didn't say that." My fingers twitched toward him and I curled them into the sleeve of my hoodie instead. Fuck, it had all been a mistake from the very beginning. "You're hurting. I know you are. At school, at home. Part of you isn't ready to deal with this thing and me being around is just making that more and more obvious to both of us. We aren't making each other's lives easier anymore, Scott. We're making them harder."

I didn't realize I was crying until he lifted a hand toward me, like he was going to pull me into him. I leaned away and wiped aggressively at my eyes.

"Don't."

"Let me," he said softly.

"No." I shook my head, almost too hard. "I don't want you to hold me."

His shoulders dropped, his eyes went misty. I hated that look. "Why not?"

"Because when you hold me I feel —" *loved* "— safe." I couldn't sit still anymore so I pushed myself off the couch and ran my hands through my hair. I was going to start sobbing if I didn't get out of there. I took another deep breath and turned to face him. "Kiss me."

"What?" Scott asked. A few tears had snuck free and he pressed his face to the corner of his elbow to wipe them away. I couldn't stop mine.

"Last time," I offered.

He frowned but stood up and crossed the distance between us. Both of his hands fit around the back of my neck, thumbs pressing just below my ears, as he tilted my head back to kiss me.

There was no fighting in this one, no teasing, no games. It was soft, sweet, and tasted salty from his tears or mine, I wasn't sure. Every part of me begged to press myself closer, to hold onto him and never let go again. But I made myself pull away, and it felt like the world was ending.

I didn't look at him as I left, I couldn't. I just jumped down the steps and went back to Rick. He had the radio playing too loud but turned it off completely once he saw me. His gaze darted from me, to the house, then back to me. "Lakyn—"

"I'm fine," I lied, and oh, how I hated to lie. "Please, take me home."

Rick didn't push, because I'd asked him not to, but I had a feeling he knew somehow, because he stopped and got me a strawberry ice cream on the way. It was really too cold outside to eat it but I didn't give a damn.

I could hear Scott's voice playing in the back of my mind. Asking *why is life so hard?* I still didn't know, but I really, really wished it wasn't.

15
"I CAN GIVE YOU THE EXACT INCHES IF YOU'RE CURIOUS!"

Kaitlynn sat with me during lunch on Monday, bringing her best friend and her little brother, neither of which I actually knew. They allowed me to fade into the background while they conversed and laughed, not pressuring me but letting me know people were there. At least until Thursday, when she got annoyed and turned to me. "Lakyn, opinion?"

"Huh?" I asked, looking up from where I was dissecting what the cafeteria was calling 'mystery meat,' I was pretty sure it was pork, but not sure enough to just dive in.

She gave me an annoyed look. "Favorite superhero."

"Oh, uh, Spider-Man," I said, then considered. "Or Deadpool."

She grinned at me. "Or Spideypool."

I shrugged at her. "Two is always better than one."

"That's what your mom said!" Kaitlynn's brother spoke up, and she put her hand on the back of his head then turned him away.

"Don't try to be cool," she scolded. "I'll make you go sit with the fishies again."

He huffed. "I'm pretty sure James here is a freshman too."

I shrugged, Kaitlynn just looked more annoyed. "Yes, but Lakyn is *actually* cool and we're lucky to be in his presence. Don't ruin it."

She was an astonishingly good bullshitter, I almost believed her. I smiled before I went back to my food and listened to them talk around me again. When the bell rang, I grabbed her wrist to hold her back, and she glanced back at me with one eyebrow raised.

"Hey. Are we friends?" I asked.

The question obviously shocked her, then her expression went sad. She nodded and tugged her hand free. "Of course, we're friends, Lakyn. I'm sorry if that wasn't clear."

I shrugged. "I was just checking."

She nodded and rushed off to class. I went slower, it was only Art, and I was just going to do homework for other classes anyway.

Matt found me during PE Friday, while I was running laps with my headphones in. Most of the class was lounging in the stands on their phones or talking their girlfriends into hand jobs behind the locker rooms; but I actually liked exercising. He caught my attention only because he lapped me, then started jogging backward.

"Show off," I accused, tugging the headphones free of my ears and looping them around my neck. "Why aren't you at practice?"

Matt rolled his eyes. "I'm not allowed to play tonight, so there's no point."

"Ew, because the whole Claire thing?"

He nodded, but for some reason didn't seem all that broken up about it, which was weird. Matt liked his football.

"I'm starting to feel like we're in some odd divorced family situation here," I said. "Like Scott and I are sharing custody of you and Kaitlynn or something."

Matt laughed in agreement and fell in beside me instead of continuing his ridiculous backwards bullshit. We both slowed our jogging to a more comfortable pace.

"Main reason I don't like it when you two fight. It's hard to juggle both of you."

"Oh, sorry, I'll try not to let my personal life inconvenience you anymore," I said.

"Asshole," he replied, then, "but hey. Guess what Scott told me last night?"

"That he has a small dick?"

"No!" Matt said immediately, then his jogging faltered. "Wait, really?"

I glanced back at him and snorted. "No, Matt, Christ."

He picked his pace back up and elbowed me. I laughed as I dodged him and

said, "Alright, fine, fine. What did he tell you?"

Matt grinned and shot a look around, like he wanted to make sure no one was close enough to hear. No one was, we were the only two on the tracks. "He said he wants to come out, man."

I stopped running. My heart was hammering in my chest and I was pretty sure it didn't have anything to do with the physical exertion. Matt stopped a few steps ahead of me, and his grin was big enough to cure my fucking depression.

"I didn't ask him to do that…"

"He didn't say you did," Matt said with a shrug. "It's been a long time coming. I'm sure it has less to do *for* you and more to do *about* you."

"I'm not sure that makes sense."

Matt shrugged again.

I took a deep breath and ran my fingers up through my hair. *Scott wanted to come out.* It was a big deal.

Matt was still grinning.

"How long have you known?" I asked. Matt was Scott's best friend, and even though the three of us hadn't discussed it, I knew he knew about me. Scott had to talk to somebody, and Matt always seemed conscious of our relationship. I'd assumed he knew Scott was gay. Or, at the very least, that Scott had talked to him about liking boys before.

"*Dude.*" He looked offended. "Since he was like, eight. I called him out about you at summer camp because someone handed him a Playboy and he didn't even stop talking about you long enough to look at it."

I cracked a smile, then actually laughed, and once Matt realized I wasn't about to lose my shit he was laughing too. We started jogging again and made it half a lap before I asked, "How is he?"

"Stressed," Matt said. "Nervous. But he's a big boy, he'll be alright."

"Yeah, he is big," I mumbled, and Matt made a disgusted sound before pushing me. I cracked up again as I stumbled a few steps in front of him, catching myself before I actually fell over.

"Dude, I really don't need to know!"

"You were very concerned earlier!" I defended, still laughing. "I can give you the exact inches if you're curious!"

Matt flipped me off and with a sudden burst of speed he was so far ahead of me I knew he wouldn't be able to hear anything I shouted at him. I chuckled, stuck my headphones back in, and took off after him.

***

When I'd been a kid and my parents would leave for weeks on end I'd found ways to entertain myself. Usually with cartoons, video games, whatever. When they'd leave and I'd been in "trouble" though, it'd gotten a lot harder. They'd take my stuff or cut the satellite or crap like that. Bridgewood only got a few local channels, and it was interesting what someone could get into when they were bored out of their mind. And hungry.

As a young teen, the cooking channel had somehow become a source of comfort. I liked the soothing voice the chefs talked with, the precise instructions, the sound of a knife on a cutting board, the finished product at the end, hard work turning into something tangible.

I hadn't bothered turning it on since I'd been at Uncle Ben's. There was no reason to when I had stuff that wouldn't be taken from me without probable cause, or when I had movies I actually enjoyed, or other people to hang out with.

But there were times when the nightmares were bad enough I didn't want to watch scary movies. And these days my razor blades were gone and I had no desire to get them back. My skin was healing, I didn't want to reopen it.

So, I ended up downstairs, wrapped in a cocoon of blankets, knees pressed into my chest and chin resting on them, watching the guy on the screen tell me how to make stuffed jalapenos. It wasn't like I'd ever actually eat them, but I couldn't sleep, and I couldn't cut, so there I was.

It was late when I heard footsteps, and I didn't bother looking because I knew it would be Juliet, headed out to another party where she would no doubt get fucked-up, then sneak right back in and no one but me would be the wiser.

"What are you doing?" Juliet asked.

"Can't sleep," I answered, "surprise, surprise."

She hesitated then walked into the room, cell phone in her hands. I tilted my head back to look at her. "Where are you going tonight?"

Her lips thinned in a way that said she didn't want to tell me, which made my stomach twist. If she didn't want to say, it probably wasn't a good idea. "I have ice cream," I offered.

"Chocolate?" she asked.

"Neapolitan."

"You're just eating the strawberry."

I picked up the half empty carton and tilted it her way in the TV light to show she was, in fact, right. The corners of her mouth quirked up and she walked away, texting something. I didn't expect her to come back, but she did, with a spoon.

I struggled out of my pile of blankets enough to let her in, and she cuddled up close and rested her head on my shoulder, happily taking the carton when I offered it to her.

"Why are you watching this?" she asked.

"I like it," I said. "It's good for my anxiety or whatever."

She hummed around a bite and shivered slightly. It was starting to get too cold out for ice cream, but neither of us really cared. "Can you cook?"

"Yeah," I said, and it almost felt like a secret for some reason. Probably because I'd been too damn lazy to make an effort lately. "For the most part. You learn, when no one's around to make you stuff."

"I haven't," she muttered. "Neither has dad. Or Rick, I'm pretty sure he lives off SpaghettiOs and takeout."

Aunt Lily had cooked. She'd loved it. Neither of us mentioned that.

"You should learn," I said instead. "It's actually fun."

Juliet put the ice cream down. "Let's make something."

"What?" I asked, glancing at her in confusion. "Right now?"

She shrugged as she stood up. "Why not? It's not like we have anything better to do."

"It's three in the morning?" I reasoned, but I was standing up myself. Juliet shrugged and led the way to the kitchen. I turned the living room TV off and picked up the carton and spoons before I followed. There was a TV in the kitchen too, a much smaller one that was used for when football games were on. I turned that on instead. "We should at least make breakfast."

Juliet shrugged. "Find us some."

"Okay." I wondered if she'd finally lost her mind. I clicked through a couple of options before I landed on a woman making Pecan Crusted French Toast. It looked good, I was pretty sure we had the ingredients, and Juliet nodded her approval.

We weren't quite sure if the spices in the cabinet had been touched since Aunt Lily died, but we also figured they didn't go bad either. At least not vanilla and cinnamon, so we used them. We ruined the first batch somehow, burnt the second, but by the third we had something that was definitely French Toast, nuts and all.

We ate it together as the sun was coming up, trying not to laugh too loud, then cleaned the kitchen so Uncle Ben and Rick would never know. It was our little secret, one that followed us through the week. And then the next.

When I woke up screaming, Juliet was the first one at the door, waving off whoever else had decided to be concerned. Then we'd go downstairs, flick through the cooking channel, and find something worth making. As the nights went by though it became obvious we couldn't do much in a house full of people that couldn't cook. We needed new materials.

Juliet wanted to go without permission, but I was still on such a short leash I refused. She'd sighed and asked her father while he was still half asleep. Anything she'd said then was met with an 'uh, sure sweetie.' It wasn't the way I preferred to go about things, but I also wanted to keep doing our nightly ritual. It kept my demons at bay and Juliet sober, so it seemed like a good thing.

We left for the grocery store at some ungodly hour of the night when people only went for alcohol and pot cravings.

Juliet didn't sneak out. And I didn't miss my razor blades.

**

It wasn't like Scott didn't exist just because we weren't talking. We had classes together, we saw each other in the hallways, Matt waved at me when they were going to lunch. I could see him, therefore I could keep an eye on him.

He was doing alright. His usual crowd was thinner, but it had been ever since the original rumors went around, and I wondered how much of that was people being dicks and how much was Scott deciding who he did and didn't want to spend time with.

There would be a grace period, and I was sure we were both aware of that, where the people he told would take a minute to adjust. His would be a lot kinder than mine had been. Scott White was a genuinely pleasant person to be around, and people liked him for him. Once they realized who he was wasn't going to change, they would come back. I was sure of it.

Matty Boy - 4:30 PM
Scott has a meeting with coach
after practice *thumbs up*

I smiled down at my phone and asked him to wish Scott good luck. The *for me* was left off, only because we both knew it would be better not to mention my name yet. Scott needed to do this, for himself, by himself. I couldn't intrude.

"You seem in good spirits," Dr. Hoar observed. I glanced up at her to see her own smile in place and shrugged.

"Maybe."

She rolled her eyes — that just caused me to grin — and pointed at me. "That's what I mean. I don't think I've seen you smile yet."

"I don't think you're in the right profession if you want to make people smile," I shot back, then I sat up straighter with a sudden thought. "Wait! No! Scratch that, I can do better, *Dr. Hoar.* Your name suggests you're in *exactly* the right profession to make people smile."

"Your uncle would hate you for that," she said, but she was laughing.

"Eh." I shrugged, unbothered. "Worth it."

She folded her clipboard under her hands before she asked, "Want to tell me what has you in such a good mood?"

The truth was, I didn't know. Sure, maybe a part of it had to do with Scott, and Juliet was still sober, had been for most of the month. She didn't partake too much when she was alone. She asked me to smoke on occasion, but I shook her off. I missed the calm that came from weed, but I was aware I needed to be good. Any small infraction could have me back on suicide watch. Rick was going out more. School wasn't awful.

I saw Dr. Hoar twice a week after class. Sometimes I talked, sometimes I didn't, but I'd put in enough of an effort that she had the majority of my backstory. She knew my scars, she knew their causes. She'd seen me scream, and cry, and kick things. She'd seen me fall apart and then put me back together before I left her office.

But she didn't know me, not really. She knew what lingered inside me.

She knew the darkness, the loneliness, the hurt. She knew the little boy curled up in the corner of my mind, crying and asking for it to stop. She was showing me how to teach him to stand on his own.

So no, my good mood wasn't because the people in my life were pulling themselves together, although I was sure that didn't hurt. It was because *I* was as well. It was because that little boy only cried at night, when it was dark and he was scared and alone.

I was getting better.

"I found a hobby," I said, instead of all that. I would, one day, when being better was permanent. For now though, it was just step one, I still had a long road ahead of me. But I was finally strong enough to walk down it.

"Yeah?" she asked.

I nodded. "I pulled Juliet into it too. Or, we pulled each other into it? I'm not entirely sure. We're cooking."

She looked impressed. "That's a good hobby to have."

Another nod. "Yeah. I thought so too. It's nice to have something to focus on, you know? Like, I used to like to put my pain behind something and ruin it. But now, I can make something instead? I don't know, it's cool."

She smiled again. "Yeah. It really is."

When I left her office I still felt good, and back home Juliet helped me with my French homework until her dad and Rick came in with stuff to make sandwiches. Everyone was happy, Juliet was cracking jokes, Uncle Ben kept catching Rick in a headlock who loudly complained he was too old for that shit.

I was safe.

I'd known since my adoption papers went through that my life was cemented, but there was something about that moment, something about us all sitting down together at the table, that finally spoke to me. *I was safe. I was safe. I was safe.*

"We should say grace, I think," Uncle Ben said before everyone started their meal. "It feels like the kind of night to say grace?"

There was a pause, because saying grace had always been Aunt Lily's thing, and she'd been the best at it. "Do you remember how it goes?" I asked, and he froze.

Juliet cleared her throat, wiped her hands off on her jeans, then held them up to us. I took one, and the others completed the circle. "Father God," she started. "Thank you for this extraordinary meal of sandwiches —" I chuckled and Uncle Ben scoffed before Rick shushed us "— Please let it nourish our bodies and something else about goodness and, uh… tell Mom we said hi. Okay. Amen."

We echoed the last word then dug into our meals, the conversation around us switched from work to school to Thanksgiving. "What do you guys want to do this year?" Uncle Ben asked, sitting back in his seat and munching on a potato chip. "I was thinking Thai and a movie, maybe?"

I wasn't sure when the last time I'd had a traditional Thanksgiving dinner was, but I knew the rest of them hadn't had one since Aunt Lily had died, no matter how many times our extended family had invited them.

"We should have turkey," I said. "And dressing. Oh, and pie."

"Funny," Rick said. "Who do you think is going to cook it? *Dad?*"

"I'm not completely useless, you know," Uncle Ben spoke up. We all chose to ignore him.

"Juliet and I can?" I offered, and glanced at my cousin for confirmation. She was surprised, but nodded in agreement.

Rick didn't seem convinced. "Since when can you two cook?"

"A lot goes on when you're not sleeping," I answered, and the double meaning was clear enough I knew he got it. Uncle Ben didn't, which was unfortunate, but not a complete loss. Especially while Juliet was doing okay.

"Alright," he said, giving in. "I want green bean casserole."

"You're weird," Juliet said.

"It's good!"

"Are you sure you want to do this?" Uncle Ben asked, arching an eyebrow. "Cooking a turkey isn't easy. Or so I've heard."

I lifted a shoulder in a shrug. "It'll keep us busy. Busy kids stay out of trouble." And without school the chances that Juliet and I would find trouble were extra high. I was definitely trying to avoid that. I turned back to her. "Macaroni?"

"Of course," she answered. "Apple pie? Mom's?"

The room went silent again, but it didn't hurt the way I thought it would. Instead, Uncle Ben smiled and turned a fond look on the wedding pictures lining the wall. "Yeah. I think I still have her recipe book."

Juliet and I shared a smile, then we went back to eating, and things were good. They were definitely good.

***

The day we were let out for Thanksgiving break, Scott White came out to the school.

16
DID YOU KNOW THERE ARE GAY PENGUINS?

Scott <3 - 10:06 AM
did u know there are gay penguins?

Me - 10:07 AM
Did you seriously wake me up for that?

Scott <3 - 10:10 AM
were u really sleeping???

Me - 10:11 AM
No. But I could have been

Me - 10:11 AM
There are more gay animals than just penguins btw

Scott <3 - 10:25 AM
omg ur right

I snorted and put my phone down, focusing my attention on *Corpse Bride*. I hadn't seen Scott, but he'd texted all through break. Whatever happened to be on his mind, just like old times. Neither of us had brought up the Coming Out incident. Yet. I was thinking about it now though.

I picked up my phone again.

Me - 10:42 AM
Hey. Remember that time you got on the announcement system at school and told everyone you were gay? That was fucking wild.

It'd happened, too. Bridgewood Academy had a tradition where they would let a student run the closing announcements right before a school break. It was usually the popular kids, they were the only ones that really cared for whatever reason, but I'd still been surprised to hear Scott's voice over the loudspeaker.

"This is Scott White. Blah blah blah a lot of stuff nobody cares about. Oh, and by the way, I'm gay. Enjoy your break! Happy Turkey Slaughter week!"

Scott <3 - 10:47 AM
yeah lol wtf was i thinking?

I honestly had no clue, and I told him as much, before I asked him how the fallout was going. Matt had texted me a few times letting me know things were better than expected. The majority of the team had taken it really well, only a few had said something dumb about the locker room situation, but that was to be expected. Scott seemed to be his usual cheery self, so I figured it was going alright. That or he was drunk. I considered asking that too, but before I did he replied.

Scott <3 - 11:00 AM
u want to come over? parents are gone, we could talk?

Scott <3 - 11:01 AM
stay the night

I dragged myself out of bed and into Juliet's room. She actually was sleeping, but I still threw myself on her. There was a grunt of displeasure from under her piles of blankets, and she jerked the covers away from her face to glare at me.

"The fuck do you want?" she asked.

"Advice," I said.

"From me?"

I hummed and rolled off the edge of her bed and back onto my feet. "Good point. I'll ask Rick."

"Yeah, right, like he'll know." She yawned and disappeared mostly under the blankets again. "What'd Scott do?"

I didn't even ask her how she knew, because usually things were about Scott. That was probably something that should have concerned me but it really didn't.

"Do you think he came out for me?"

The blanket pile moved in a shrug. "Even if he did, he would have done it eventually."

"Maybe." I scratched at the back of my neck. "Do you think I should go talk to him?"

"Do you want to?"

"Yes."

She rolled over, getting more comfortable. "Then I think you have your answer."

"Jules."

"What?"

"I need you to drive me."

"I'm sleeping."

I left her alone to go call my uncle instead. He and Rick didn't get a weeklong break like we did, they were back at work, but I knew he wouldn't be too busy. He answered on the third ring with a quick, *'what's up?'*

"Hey," I said. "Do you care if I spend the night at Scott's place?"

"I didn't think you like the Whites that much?"

"I don't," I admitted. I didn't say *'they won't be there.'* It wasn't technically a lie, just an omission of truth.

"Are you good? Nightmares-wise?"

I wasn't waking up screaming as much anymore, but I still couldn't make it through the night. Unfortunately, that was a fact everyone knew. "Honesty, we probably won't sleep. Scott has a shit ton of video games and it's not like we have to be anywhere in the morning. It'll be like camp, no big."

"Alright," he said. "No parties. No alcohol. No drugs. If I suspect even for a second —"

"I promise," I interrupted. He didn't ask if we were fucking and I didn't offer up that information either. It wasn't like I even really knew anymore.

***

Scott looked good. Which wasn't surprising because he usually did. But there was something different. It was like he used to slouch and finally had learned how to stand up straight. Something small, but noticeable, something I couldn't name but that was definitely there.

"Are you drunk?"

"What?" Scott asked, blinking like he hadn't heard me correctly. "Oh, no. I was the first couple days of break, though."

Wasn't that, then. He moved out of his doorway to let me in and I crossed it slowly, like I was waiting for something to jump out and yell April Fools. The world just felt surreal somehow. Like all of this couldn't possibly be happening.

"You want a drink, though?" Scott asked. "Food? Pot?"

"I quit," I said. "Hoping Juliet will follow in my footsteps. Soda?"

I wasn't really thirsty but I figured I could use something to do with my hands, and Scott gave a nod before twisting off into the kitchen. I went to the living room instead. It was too clean, in a way that meant his parents had just left, although his Xbox was pulled out and Matt's username was flashing across the screen, meaning they'd probably been talking before I got there. I swiped up the controller, fell onto the couch, and started a game of Halo before he came back.

He pulled out another controller without prompting and sat on the floor. For a while that was all we did. Just got used to being back in each other's presence.

"Why did you do it?" I finally asked.

"You pretty much told me to get my shit together or you were gone. I mean, you were already gone, but that's what the whole splitting up thing was about, wasn't it? I was a mess, and you couldn't be with a mess."

I pressed my lips together and didn't look away from the screen. It was true, in a way, even though that hadn't been exactly how I'd meant for it to come across. I'd just wanted things to be easier for both of us. "I didn't ask you to come out for me."

"True, you didn't. But you deserved for me to," Scott said. He hesitated long enough for me to sneak up behind him in the game and kill him, which earned me a swear then silence while he respawned and got his bearings back. "I want to be with you, Lake. But it's not fair of me to ask you to shove yourself back in the closet. To make yourself smaller or less than. So, here I am."

I nodded and chewed on my bottom lip. "So, you did it for yourself?"

"Yeah," he said, "I was scared. I was scared of being different, or losing my friends, or having things fall apart around me. But really, I think at this point, this is who I am. I'm Scott White, and I'm hella gay, and that's okay."

"True."

He chuckled softly before catching me completely off guard in the game with a sniper shot. I frowned and gave him a look, but his stupidly bright smile was nice enough I didn't mind losing the round. Fucker.

"Coach took it better than expected too," Scott said. "He was all *'why are you telling me this'* until I pointed out that I wanted to tell the team. He and Matt had my back there. It... wasn't awful."

I let that sit for a minute while we played, and we got through a few rounds more seriously than we had been before. Then I asked, "And the fucking announcement?"

Scott laughed in a way that said he still wasn't one-hundred-percent comfortable with that brilliant move. "I didn't plan it. I don't know, there I was with a whole week of break in front of me, and after everything else I'd just done it seemed so fucking dumb to still be in the closet. So I just ripped the damn Band-Aid off and walked away. I figure everyone can use the break to get over it."

"Fair enough."

Scott lifted a shoulder. "I haven't told my parents yet. I… that's… I don't know…"

"Terrifying?" I supplied. I remembered. Vividly. "You're going to have to soon. The whole school knows, someone else might tell them."

He paused the game then in order to look up at me, and I was struck again by just how young he looked, which was ridiculous because he was a year older than me, but right then it didn't seem like it. Scott was just a boy, who had his fair share of hardships but was mostly untouched by the cruelties of the world. If it hadn't been for the gay thing, he would have been forever unhurt by things. What a messed up situation. "I'm sorry this is so hard for you."

"Aren't the good things worth the struggle?" he asked.

"I don't know," I admitted. "I'll fill you in when I find out."

He nodded like that was a fair answer, and continued to look at me for a while before taking a deep breath. He turned his gaze to the TV, out the window, at the ceiling, then finally back at me. "So, what do you think? I know you don't fuck your friends, and I know you don't do boyfriends, but maybe… would you want to make another exception, just this once?"

"For you?" I asked.

He gave me an incredibly unamused look. "No, Ryan Gosling. Yes, for me, you little shit."

"I *would* date Ryan Gosling," I muttered.

"I fucking know you would."

I laughed and rolled off the couch and right into his lap. He made a sound of discomfort but still managed to catch me, glaring slightly with a nervous pink tinge to his cheeks. I wrapped my arms around his neck and pulled him in for a quick kiss. "You know me," I warned. "The good, the bad, the ugly. You have all the cards. Are you sure you want to do this?"

Scott rolled his eyes. "Shut up and kiss me again."

I grinned, and did as I was told.

***

Scott and I spent the day together and it was good. Easy. A mixture of video games, throwing food at each other from opposite ends of the couch, and scary movies that we made out through. I laughed, and Scott laughed, and I twined my fingers through his with the knowledge that I wouldn't have to stop any time soon.

We talked. About us, about the future, for hours upon hours. Until eventually I was too damn tired to keep it going anymore. We brushed our teeth and changed into pajamas and I realized I hadn't had a decent minute of sleep since the last time I'd been next to him.

"I talk a lot of shit, but you know I think you're kind of amazing, right?"

I asked when we climbed into bed.

"You mean, do I know that *'you're an idiot'* translates to *'holy fuck, I like you a lot'*? Yes. I speak Lakyn."

"Shut up," I muttered, and rolled my eyes at his stupid smile.

He let me curl up close and I drifted away to the warmth of his body and the smell of his shampoo and the reality that I was fine. It was perfect.

Until it wasn't.

I didn't know when or how my father had gotten there but I felt his harsh grip against the back of my neck. My stomach twisted and my heart pounded me awake and I knew Scott was still there — if I could only hold onto him. My fingers scraped for purchase, someone was screaming, my mind was a broken record of *Scott, Scott, Scott.*

Oh, it was me. I was screaming.

My shoulder hit the wall hard enough I heard something crack and I turned my head as I waited for the punch to come. My blood was rushing quick enough I could fucking hear it. My adrenaline was on high. What had I done?

The hit never came.

It took me a while to recognize the woman I was seeing in the hallway as Scott's mother. Her eyes were wide and glassy, her hand over her heart, and she was staring at me like I was somewhere I shouldn't be. Where was my father?

No.

This wasn't my room, it was Scott's. And it wasn't my dad, it was *Scott's*.

Scott was out of bed and in his father's space, face twisted up in anger, pushing at him. His father was yelling, slapping his hands away, I couldn't make out what he was saying though because Scott was talking over him.

"Don't you ever fucking touch him again! Don't you ever!"

The longer I realized I wasn't in my parents' house, the more the panic faded into something manageable. I took deep, calming breaths as I watched Scott push until they were both in the hallway, then I took a step forward to keep an eye on them. They'd forgotten I was there, and I was selfishly grateful about it.

His mother was crying now, reaching for them then changing her mind halfway there. "Scott, Scott stop it!" her voice was choked and her makeup was ruined.

My hands were shaking.

"I raised a boy, a man!" Scott's father was saying, finger pointed in his son's face. "Not a fucking *fag*."

"Stop it!" his mother said again, and she reached for Scott's face but he jerked just out of her touch. Her fingers wrung together in midair instead. "It's okay darling, it's okay! We'll get you help and it'll be fine. Y-you're sick, but you can get better! There are places for that. Camps! We'll send you to one! It'll be fine!"

Scott looked up and caught my eye. I could see the pain written all over his face. They'd pulled me out of his bed, but somehow they'd managed to pull his heart out too. He was breaking. This was everything he'd been afraid of, thrown in his face.

I licked my lips and took in how brown his eyes were, how much I loved the shape of his mouth, how he knew his parents were saying things but he was looking at *me*. Like I was the eye of his storm. Like I was his comfort zone.

Like I could save him.

"I love you." I mouthed it slowly, carefully, so there would be no doubt between what he saw and what I meant. I felt it in every fiber of my being. I would go to the end of the world for that boy. I would do whatever he needed. I would be there for him.

His expression cleared and he moved back into his bedroom, ripping open a dresser drawer and tossing a hoodie and a pair of pajama pants my way. I jerked them on over my boxers while keeping a close eye on his father. Apparently, Scott's earlier outburst had done enough to keep him from crossing the threshold this time.

"What are you doing?" Mr. White demanded. "What the fuck are you doing!"

Scott slammed the drawer shut, stepped into his shoes, snagged the Jeep's keys off the side table, then held his hand out to me. I hesitated but took it, twining our fingers together tightly. I watched his father wind up once more, his nostrils flaring.

"Scott Alexander White —"

"Shut up," Scott interrupted. His voice was calm, factual, leaving no room for argument. "And move."

Mr. White shuffled back like he wasn't sure why, but he did. Scott put me in front of him and I tried my best to control my breathing. The real threat wasn't here, and this guy wasn't actually a problem. He wouldn't *really* hurt me.

Scott kept us walking and Mr. White followed, stuttering out an array of *'stop right now, young man!'* and *'where the hell do you think you're going?'*. Scott didn't stop until his father grabbed his arm, then he asked in a low, dangerous voice, "Are you going to throw me around too?"

His father let us go then, out the door, to the driveway, into the Jeep. Scott sat there for a moment and took two deep breaths before reversing out. It was a quiet drive, and he did it with one hand on the wheel and the other holding mine and a little too fast.

It was past midnight when we got to my place, but the lights were still on in the living room. I could hear someone laughing and I sighed as I used my key in the front door and let us in. My cousins and my uncle were playing some complicated board game, but the time of night alerted all of them to my entrance.

"Lakyn?" Rick asked, obviously confused, but Uncle Ben's attention was on Scott, and I knew that he knew exactly what sort of situation we were in. His mouth thinned and he cleared his throat before saying, "I think you two should give us a moment."

Juliet and Rick both climbed to their feet. Juliet squeezed my shoulder on her way to the kitchen. I watched her go with an uncomfortable tugging in my chest. What had started out as the best day was ending a lot more difficult than it should have.

"What happened?" Uncle Ben asked, and the tone of his voice said this wasn't a time for half-truths. "Did your parents kick you out?"

"No," Scott answered, then considered, and his grip on my hand tightened almost painfully. "Um, there were talks about getting help. About camps."

My uncle turned to me. "I thought you were staying the night at a friend's."

I winced.

"To be fair," Scott cut in. "We were just friends. Until today."

Half-truth, but at least it wasn't my half-truth. "Now we're something more," I offered.

"I can see that." Uncle Ben sighed and got to his feet as well. He motioned Scott in for a hug and to my surprise, Scott actually went. He clung to my uncle and I watched his shoulders heave with tears he couldn't hold back any more.

Not for the first time lately, I wondered why life was so fucking hard.

"You can stay here," Uncle Ben said, just like I knew he would. "We can get your things tomorrow. I'll go with you to talk to your parents, if you want me to."

Scott didn't say anything, but he did nod, then he asked to take a shower and I walked with him. When he was good, I recounted the events at Scott's in my own words to my uncle as we put sheets on the couch together and everyone got ready to call it a night. The night had taken a toll on us all, not just the people directly involved.

When it was all said and done, I lay in bed, uncomfortable in my own skin, tossing and turning until well past two in the morning. Scott was still awake when I went into the living room, and I mentally yelled at myself for thinking even for a minute that we could sleep apart after all that.

I should have just asked.

When Scott lifted the blanket I slid right up next to him, resting my head on his chest and letting him bury his fingers in my hair. For the second time that night I fell asleep, lulled by his heartbeat.

17
"YOU'RE GOING TO BE OKAY."

I woke up because I felt like someone was staring at me and I'd never been a fan of that. Scott was still asleep, his arm wrapped loosely around my waist, and I smiled slightly before I twisted around enough to look behind me.

My uncle was standing just beside the couch, his arms folded over his chest, expression unreadable but tense. I winced, because I'd meant to be back in my own room before he'd gotten up. I was always the first one awake, it shouldn't have been hard.

"It's noon," he said, like he could read my mind, and my entire world shifted in an instant. I'd never slept until noon before. He used his head to motion for me to follow him, and I gently detangled myself from Scott before going into the kitchen. I was still wearing his hoodie and his pajama pants, and the comfort of his smell clung to me.

"Noon?" I repeated.

Uncle Ben nodded and got out the stuff to make a sandwich. I worked my fingers up under my sleeve to trace at my scars before following his lead and going for some cereal. We were quiet while we worked on our meals, then I hopped up on the counter and gave him my attention. I wasn't sure what was coming.

"Did you know that this is the first time since you've been here that you haven't woken up from a nightmare? Not once. You slept all night long."

I paused with my spoon halfway to my mouth, realizing he was right. I never did have nightmares when Scott was around. There was something about the way he held me when I slept, something about having him there, that felt safe.

My uncle sipped his soda. When he spoke again, it reminded me of our talk after my drugged-up accident. No lies, no secrets, just facts. "You're too comfortable with him for a thing that only started yesterday."

I took a deep breath and let it out slowly. "I wouldn't let it be anything more, before. I wouldn't let him call it anything more. I didn't want it to be serious, because I was afraid he couldn't handle it. No — that he couldn't handle *me*. I didn't want to ruin him."

"But it is serious." It wasn't a question, but I nodded anyway, and my uncle did too before he went back to his food. "How long have you been having sex?"

I figured *'who said I was?'* wasn't the right answer, so I chewed my food thoughtfully and went with, "Since before Scott. Before I moved in here."

Uncle Ben gave me another nod. "You know, me and my siblings never had a lot of rules growing up. Our parents trusted us, maybe too much, but they did. As long as no one was hurt, we were cool. I've tried to extend that same practice with my kids. Maybe it's working, maybe it's not, I don't know. I'm still learning, and more so with you. A lot of parents would judge me for letting you sleep with him all night."

"The sex thing?" I guessed.

He shrugged. "Among other issues. But to be honest, I don't think they're particularly important right now. You *slept*, Lakyn. All night long, for the first time in almost a year, you slept."

"I did," I whispered. I understood the importance of it, I saw it in the group of gray hairs at his temples, in the lines around his eyes. He was fucking tired too.

We were both exhausted, and now that I had rested, I could see how deep it went.

He took a step toward me and I didn't have to be asked before I leaned into his hold, pressing my face against his shoulder and sighing as his arms went around me. It was what hugging my father should have always been like. It was acceptance.

"You're going to be okay."

"Yeah," I said. "I think I am."

***

My uncle drove Scott home around dinner time. The theory was that he would stay there if he could, and come back if he couldn't. I wanted to go, but Uncle Ben thought it would be best if I wasn't there to sway Scott's feelings, and Scott thought it would be best if I wasn't around all that yelling. Neither point I could actually argue with.

Juliet curled up with me on the couch and I let her paint my nails while we watched movies. She didn't ask, but I told her about what had happened anyway. I kept my phone in my lap in case Scott called or texted, but he didn't. I had no idea what was going on.

It was late before my uncle got back, and he came in with a sour expression and two duffel bags swung over his shoulder.

"Oh no," Juliet muttered, untangling herself from me before Scott came through the door. He was trying to be his normal self, loaded down with bags too, but when he focused on me his mask dropped.

Everything dropped. His shoulders, his bags, and I stood up just in time for him to burrow into my arms. It was weird being the stronger one of the two of us, but I knew I could handle it. For him.

Uncle Ben caught my eye and shook his head slowly. The fact that Scott was here at all meant it hadn't gone as desired, but that head shake said it had been worse than expected.

"You alright?" I whispered.

"No," Scott answered with a sigh. "Are we watching movies?"

I nodded and Juliet opened her arms, so Scott switched me for her, cuddling up against her side while I grabbed his bags and took them up to my room. My uncle was there putting down the ones he had been carrying, and we shared a look before he nodded and clasped my shoulder.

When I got back to the others I climbed onto the couch and made it work by draping myself over their legs. Scott pulled me up to right under his chin, clasping his hands around my chest, and we lay like that until well into the middle of the night, with us surrounding him and keeping him whole.

Eventually I realized none of us were going to be sleeping, and I tilted my head back to look at him and ask, "Hey. You want to make an apple pie?"

Scott choked on a surprised laugh. "What?"

Juliet perked up. "Mom's pie?"

I nodded and rolled off the couch, pulling the other two with me and leading the way into the kitchen. Juliet dug for Aunt Lily's old cookbook while I pulled out the ingredients we still had left over. It was about three in the morning, but no one would care.

"It'll make you feel better," I promised Scott, pressing a kiss to his cheek. He shrugged in a way that said he wasn't going to argue. His eyes were wet, but his smile was real, and I squeezed his hand before grabbing the dough and showing him how to knead the crust with his knuckles.

We were going to be okay.

***

"What do you think the gay penguins do all day?"

I snorted and looked up at Scott from across the kitchen table. It'd been a week since he'd moved in, his shit still wasn't unpacked, but he was making it.

School was messy. The fact that Scott White was gay had been widely accepted, but it'd changed things. Some people were cruel, or distant, the latter of which Scott preferred. For the most part though, he was still the dude that everyone seemed to like.

He admitted that he didn't mind his usual boisterous crowd downsizing. Matt and Kaitlynn of course stayed close, and Juliet surprisingly joined in after break. Apparently, she wasn't feeling her usual pack of deviants. It made me hopeful.

"Gay penguins?" Rick asked, confused and a bit put out. The addition of yet another damaged teen under his roof was causing some strain, but that was to be expected. Surprisingly, Juliet was holding it together, even though now her father's attention was spread out even more.

"He's obsessed. Don't ask. He'll talk forever," I said.

Scott grinned at me. "Don't act like you don't find it cute."

I flipped him off and Juliet sighed. "Not at the table."

"I didn't say anything!"

She shot me a look that stated I didn't have to say anything at all, and Scott's smirk agreed.

"Boys," my uncle sighed, and I laughed hard enough to diffuse the tension.

Midweek Uncle Ben had set both of us down and given us a clear and pointed sex talk. If Scott and I were going to be having sex in his house — which we were, he knew that, we knew that — the rules were that we had to be practicing it as safely as possible. He made us do the research, answer questions, find out how to get tested and where. We had a lot of hard talks about sex and about responsibility. He made it very clear that he didn't want us parading our sex life around anymore than we would want to see him do the same. It was awkward, but we both understood the importance of acting like adults if we wanted to be treated like adults.

He ended the conversation with, "But please don't have sex in my kitchen," and for some reason it'd turned into an ongoing joke.

I was also looking at an entire week staying nightmare free, since Scott was allowed in my bed. He'd asked Uncle Ben about the sleeping arrangements once, claiming that it never would have been allowed in his house. He'd lived in a "no girls in your room, no closed doors" situation.

My uncle had simply shrugged and said, "Lakyn has been through a lot. You have been through a lot. I remember what it was like to be a teenage boy, and you're going to do whatever you want to do anyway. As o right now, you two are supporting each other and providing a stability I can't. If this is what it takes for you to both be okay, then this is what it takes. It's not a battle worth fighting."

That logic wasn't something either of us could — or wanted to — dispute, so we didn't. We left it alone. We knew what we needed, and that happened to be each other. Across the table I smiled at him, and he smiled back.

Juliet, Scott and I had cooked dinner, so Rick and Uncle Ben cleaned up after. It was starting to be a bit of a tradition, actually. Anytime one of us felt the need to dive into our vices, we made something instead. Scott got onto us eventually for baking too many sweets and put us on a healthier meal plan. Juliet and I grumbled about it, but it wasn't a bad idea in the long run.

Scott and I went back to my room for homework, though neither of us were being very diligent. He was lying across my bed on his stomach, my head was resting on the small of his back, and things felt — good.

"Hey, do you remember what a dick you were at summer camp?"

I snorted and rolled over, dropping my book somewhere unimportant. My fingers went to the sliver of skin showing where his shirt had rolled up, just happy to touch him. "You were the one who threw a football at my face."

"Matt threw it," he corrected.

I hummed and drew my thumb down, catching it in the waist of his pants. "You missed it on purpose."

He hesitated long enough that I knew I was right, and a smile curled on the edges of my mouth before he finally muttered, "True."

"You would have felt really bad if I hadn't caught it."

"I would have offered to kiss it and make it better."

I laughed and pushed his shirt up further, tracing the knobs of his spine and leaning down to ghost my breath across his skin. He shifted slightly, stretching out, and I glanced up to see him fold his arms under his head, which was tilted like he was trying to watch what I was doing.

"I never expected you to call me out on my flirting," he said.

"Yeah, well, you weren't exactly coy about it." I dipped my tongue into one of the dimples in the small of his back and smiled when he sighed, moving to do the same to the other.

"You say that like it hadn't been working. It'd totally been working."

"True," I admitted, and slid my hand under the back of his jeans to get a good grip of his ass. It was an awkward angle but I didn't mind too much. "This helps."

"You're a pain," he said. "Gonna do anything fun while you're down there?"

"Nah." I pulled my hand free and leaned forward to nip at the base of his neck. "I'm studying."

Scott laughed and twisted away so he could lift up on his knees and jerk his shirt off over his head. I moved onto my back and grinned up at him. "What exactly do you think is about to happen here? Do you think I'm easy?"

Scott rolled his eyes. "Lakyn James, nothing about you is *'easy.'* Now take your shirt off."

"Sir yes sir." I shimmied out of it before he leaned down to kiss me Spider-Man style. It wasn't nearly as simple as it looked in the movies, and I couldn't stop fucking smiling even as I worked on undoing my pants.

We tried until he started laughing and pulled away to get off the bed to jerk his jeans down while I kicked mine off. I made grabby hands for him and he shook his head but fell down over me, his mouth going for my neck. I happily tilted my head back to give him more room, laughing when his fingers dug into the sensitive spot below my ribs. "Stop it!"

"Why?" he asked innocently, trailing kisses until he got to my chest, then continuing down all the way to my navel. Usually he didn't notice the scars anymore, but if he did, they always got some kind of attention. He dug his fingers in again and I jerked before giving another laugh.

"I like that sound," he muttered into my hip bone.

"Asshole," I said, and amused brown eyes peeked up at me before he left my side alone in favor of snapping the waistband of my boxers. I lifted my hips for him to drag them off, but he just went back to kissing me instead. "Scott."

"Lakyn."

"*Scott.*"

He folded an arm over my stomach and rested his chin on it, giving me his undivided attention. "Yes, dear?"

I glared up at the ceiling. "You fucking tease."

"I learned from the best," he said and shifted between my legs to get more comfortable. My breath hitched at the friction and I reached a hand down to curl in his hair. I needed him. I always needed him. I could never seem to get enough.

"Please."

He smirked and went back to kissing my skin, running his mouth between my inner thighs but promptly avoiding the one part of me that was still clothed. I whimpered and tried to tug his head down but he was having none of it, preferring to lick across the lines of newly appearing abs, running his nose up my side, rolling his hips down into mine. I relaxed under his attention, nothing more than melted bones and *wantwantwant*.

"Scott. Scott," I whined, arching my back, trying to make him give me more. "Please. Baby, *please.*"

He grinned the stupidest, brightest damn smile I'd ever seen and it took me a moment to realize I'd used a damn pet name on him. "Oh my god. You nerd."

"You said it," he muttered, leaning forward to press his mouth to mine. He was still smiling too much. "You called me '*baby.*'"

"I'll call you that for the rest of our lives if you'll just fucking — *oh.*" I cut off the second his hand was on my dick, gripping his shoulder at the sudden wave of pleasure. "Asshole."

There was a part of me that felt like this was a game that I had to win, but as he leaned in to kiss me again I realized I didn't. Scott was mine. He wasn't going anywhere. This was something I could finally have without worrying that it would be taken away. We were all in. Together.

He worked at me until the world fell into place with what was going on in my head, like everything would remain perfect and blissful forever, like nothing else existed but *this* and *him* and *touch*. Scott broke our kiss and chuckled when I huffed at him.

"What?" I asked, irritated.

"You can't stop smiling."

I rolled my eyes and he pressed his forehead to mine, grinning like a fucking hypocrite. "No. It's a good thing."

"You're such a sap sometimes."

He lifted a shoulder and kissed the tip of my nose. "We got all wrapped up in this and I'm not sure where my lube is."

He was supposed to take care of this crap.

I whined pitifully and pushed his head away so I could cover my face. "Why are you so mean to me?"

"You're such a drama queen," he said as he rolled off the bed completely. I glared and watched him open bag after bag, making a complete fucking mess.

"This would be a lot easier if you would just unpack, you freak."

"I said I will later," Scott muttered, and my stomach did a stupid little flip over 'later'. Because there would be a later. We didn't have to rush this anymore. "That was last week."

"Well it's still not 'later' yet," he said, and smiled at me as he finally found what he was looking for. He grabbed a condom before he got back on the bed, settling down on my thighs. I folded my arms up under my head to watch him, but he put both things down and leaned forward, catching himself on his elbows on either side of my head. Bright eyes looked into mine, and my heart stuttered before he said, "Hey. I love you."

He fucking meant it too, and I let him kiss me again, slow and soft and filled with things he couldn't quite put into words yet. It was all too much and I couldn't really handle it. So, when he pulled back I cracked a smile. "Yeah, baby, I know. You gonna fuck me now? Or do you wanna *make love*?"

"You are *such* a little shit," Scott said, dropping his forehead on my chest before we both cracked up laughing.

And yeah. We were okay.

EPILOGUE
LIVING WAS DEFINITELY WORTH IT.

December was almost over when I walked into Dr. Hoar's office and started talking the moment the door shut behind me. It was like once I opened my mouth I couldn't fucking stop. Word vomit, everywhere. I couldn't even sit down, I just started pacing.

"The first time I really remember being in pain, I was five. My teacher had told me that my drawing was really cool and asked if I was excited to show my mom. When I shook my head she'd pressed me for-fucking-ever on why. Apparently 'she doesn't like me' wasn't a good enough answer. She kept telling me I was wrong. All mothers love their little boys. So, like an idiot, I believed her. I went home and followed my mother around while she was getting ready, babbling on and on about this stupid, pointless drawing of a flower or something, I don't even remember. She kept telling me to go away, I was annoying her. When I didn't, she grabbed me by the hair and pressed her curling iron into my bare shoulder."

I took a deep breath and Dr. Hoar arched an eyebrow at me before crossing one leg over the other and motioning for me to keep going. I wasn't sure if I wanted to. Every nerve in my body protested, screaming at me to *shut up*, but I pressed on.

"They were only violent if they remembered that I was there. Uncle Ben always hated how neglectful they were but I didn't really mind. If I was quiet, if I snuck home, if I stayed in my room, then no one hit me. But no one remembered to feed me, either, so it was usually a game of 'what's worse'. My clothes never fit, my hair was never cut, and Aunt Lily had to teach me how to bathe myself because I was never clean until I was like, fucking seven years old.

I changed schools after kindergarten, have I mentioned that? Switched to Bridgewood Academy. I found out in middle school that my uncle was paying for it, even though my parents definitely had the money. I'm pretty sure he paid them too. Who knows what they did with the extra cash.

Bought drugs probably. He moved me so he could keep an eye on me, I'm sure of it. Didn't stop my father from beating the shit out of me, though. Hey! Did you know my doctor never asked why I was always in such awful shape? Maybe *that's* what they were doing. Paying him off."

She made a face at that. "You have a new one now, right?"

"Sure," I waved off the question because technically I didn't, but if the need ever arose my uncle would take care of it. He took care of a lot of stuff. Way more than he should. I crossed the room and shrugged off my hoodie, then pulled my shirt up over my head, so I could trail my fingers over the scars on my arms.

I tapped against the mismatched lines on my right bicep. "I had a panic disorder by ten, self-diagnosed, but you know. I'd get all dizzy and couldn't breathe and my ears would start ringing. I couldn't live like that and pretty soon I figured out pain made it stop. It grounded me, I guess. It started with a pocketknife, that's why some of these are so much wider. It wasn't mine. I stole it off my friend's big brother. When he found out he traded me for a pack of razor blades. They worked better. Thinner lines."

"So, that's when the cutting started?" she asked.

I nodded. "You know what happens to kids' minds when they don't have anyone to talk to? At all? They start keeping it all inside and then it fucks with their heads."

"What about your aunt and uncle?"

I leveled her with a look. "I wasn't supposed to bother them."

She waited me out until I grit my teeth and dragged my blunt nails across the scars on my arm, leaving angry but temporary red lines behind. "My parents made it clear that if I leaned on my aunt and uncle too much, I'd never see them again. When I threatened to run away, my mother promised we'd get on a plane and go so far I'd never figure out how to get back. They were all I had. It terrified me."

Dr. Hoar nodded, like that was a deep enough explanation, then asked, "What about your teachers?"

I laughed and shook my head, then started pacing again. "I told two teachers I needed help. Once in elementary, once in middle school. The first one made the mistake of telling my parents I should get some real counseling. My dad was very unhappy about that. I got some nice bruises for it."

I expected her to wince, but she didn't. It was like she knew that if she reacted badly now, I'd clam up. Joke was on her though, I couldn't. My hands were shaking and my heart was pounding but my mouth wouldn't stop moving. "The second one called CPS. Downside is that if things look normal CPS can't help you. My house growing up *always* looked normal. People liked my parents. They were upstanding citizens. Good Christians. Clean and tidy. I learned real fucking fast how to become invisible after that. I learned that I was alone. No one was going to believe me. No one was going to help me."

I stopped walking and stretched my arm out to look at the scars there again. I could pick out the ones that were self-inflicted and the ones that weren't. The ones that came from staged accidents and the ones that were real. "You know, the thing about emotional pain is that it's all in here —" I started to point at my head then thought better of it and pressed my hand to my heart instead. "No one can look at me and see how fucking much I was left alone, or how fucking awful it was. Do you know how many times I passed out because I was hungry? My parents aren't poor, for Christ's sake."

Maybe that was why the cutting had gotten so out of control. Maybe I wanted someone to *see*, at least subconsciously. Maybe I wanted someone to notice. Ironic, given the lengths I went to cover the scars. I wanted to kick something but I closed my eyes and took a deep breath instead. I tried to count to ten but I couldn't make it all the way through. I had more things to say.

"I got hit for everything. Good grades? Backhanded for being a 'goddamn know-it-all'. Bad grades? Black eye for being an idiot. I couldn't ever win. Smacked for talking too much, yelled at for being too quiet. Thirsty? No big, son, we'll just fill the sink up and try to *fucking drown you in it*."

I walked across the room to press my forehead to the window glass. Dr. Hoar followed me with her eyes, but she never said anything. I took a few calming, deep breaths but it didn't help much. Anxiety was creeping in, but something was lifting off of me, too. Like I was dropping weight I'd been carrying for years without realizing it.

This was helping, even though it hurt.

"My only solace ever was at my aunt and uncles, but then Aunt Lily died… and the entire world shifted. I couldn't lean on them anymore because they were like a table missing a leg, you know? The support's still there but any extra pressure in the wrong place and it'll collapse. So I kept to myself. And the thing about keeping to yourself, about not talking, about handling it all alone… is that you start to regret it any time you do say something. The words leaving your mouth are like poison. They make you physically sick, and the next thing you know you're digging a blade into your thighs to ease the pressure a little bit. Because that's the only thing you have control over."

Not for the first time, I stared out Dr. Hoar's window and watched the cars go by, wondering about the people in them. How many were normal? How many were on their phones with their mothers, crying because their spouses beat them and they wanted out? How many kids were too silent, because they'd learned crying didn't work? How many were broken?

"That kind of loneliness is bone-deep," I muttered, and my heart slowed. Out of exhaustion or something else, I wasn't sure. "It wears at your soul until you have to hurt yourself a little more just to make sure three months don't pass by when you blink. It makes you start having sex too young because you think that'll make you feel wanted. Until you can't even remember the names or the faces but that's okay. It's not a big deal. It feels good, so it must be helping, right? It makes you pop pills until you stop feeling at all. Until you don't need to be wanted, or loved, or cared for anymore."

I pushed myself off the window and turned my back toward it instead, my fingers pressing at the scars on my wrist. They were forever going to be a reminder of how low I'd fallen, of a time when I'd given up.

"It makes you so damn tired that you just decide to stop trying. What's it worth anyway? Life is hard and unfair and everyone just fucking loves to remind you of that. Over and over and over again. Until you just... don't want to do it anymore. Because there's no end in sight."

Dr. Hoar pointed her pen at me. "But you're still here."

I nodded.

"And you're not going anywhere."

I shook my head, even though it wasn't really a question, and looked at the scars on my wrist one more time. I'd survived. I wasn't going to try to kill myself, not again.

"Why not?" she asked.

"I'll let you know when I figure it out."

***

The day after New Year's, Juliet and I got into a car crash, and it hadn't even really been her fault. She'd taken a turn, some jackass hadn't been paying attention, and he'd rammed into us. Totaled her car, deployed both airbags, gave her a nasty case of whiplash, and broke my right arm.

I'd been furious, and with no one else to direct that anger at, I'd turned it on her. Screaming about how she could have fucking killed me, cradling my hurt arm to my chest, angrier than I'd been in a long damn time.

Julie had only laughed; a crazed, high-pitched sound that came from shocked adrenaline. Which had made me even more mad. I'd slammed my palm against the cracked dash and asked her *what the hell she thought was so goddamned funny.*

She'd looked at me through tears and a wobbly smile before saying, "Lakyn. You want to be alive."

It was a real interesting turning point for me. I couldn't recall the day that I'd stopped wanting to be dead, but I had. At some point, the world around me had become good enough that I wanted to be a part of.

We both took a while to recover from that damn wreck but it didn't bother me too bad for some reason. Like I'd needed it to happen to understand that I was finally where I'd been trying to get all year.

I started taking Driver's Ed because Uncle Ben made it clear that he wasn't going to allow Juliet to drive again for a while. She was down three cars and he was sick of it. I didn't really mind, I was behind anyway, and I got a small black truck for my seventeenth birthday present. It represented trust and independence and a milestone I never thought I would have reached. I loved it.

I drove Scott to our first 'official date' in that truck, and then let him blow me in it later. To be fair, I'd started it. An empty theater had proved too tempting and I'd been too wound up. If no one was there to see a blowjob in action, was it really public sex?

Juliet fell back into old habits eventually, and while I'd seen it coming, it still fucking sucked to watch it happen. In June she got picked up for vandalism. Some stupid spray paint on the side of a building. The owner knew Uncle Ben through various car deals, so he promised not to press charges, as long as Juliet cleaned it up. Her father made her do it alone, then he finally caved and admitted to what I'd been trying to tell him all along.

Unlike my stubborn ass, Juliet chose in-patient treatment — a couple of months to get her off the drugs and some intense grief counseling. Little by little, each time I visited her, she seemed more like herself. She was tired and emotionally exhausted, but I knew what that was like. One particularly hard day led to her crying with her head in my lap while we talked about Aunt Lily. Something we hadn't ever really let ourselves do.

"You remember what she used to say to us?" Juliet asked softly.

"That we're loved infinitely," I replied, the memory clear enough that she could have been there. Somehow, that phrase was more powerful then than it had ever been before. If anything had proved I was loved, it was the last year. I had my uncle, my cousins, Scott, and friends that all cared about me and my wellbeing.

And she did too. We would help keep each other whole.

I brought up the idea of tattoos to Uncle Ben and his mouth became thin, but a few days later, Rick gave me the name of a friend and when Juliet got discharged we inked tiny infinity symbols into our wrists. As a reminder to never forget again. We were loved infinitely.

As it had a bad fucking habit of doing, school got nasty. Juliet had been gone long enough that her reappearance was like striking a match on the rumor mill.

The stories ranged from the fact that she'd run away to have a baby, to having an abortion, to rehab (which was true, but everyone's drug of choice was heroin, which wasn't true), to becoming a porn star. She was a straight girl playing games, or a lesbian who couldn't keep her skirt on, or anything and everything in between.

She didn't fit in Bridgewood Academy anymore, I wasn't sure she ever had, but she was determined not to let anyone run her out. By winter break, she cracked. She pulled everything out of her closet, stripped her bed, dumped out her jewelry, and donated it all. "I hate tight clothes," she'd said, then sent her barefoot into her perfect white dresser. "And I hate white."

I'd laughed so hard it'd almost hurt and took her shopping. We got clothes that were a bit too big but that she'd loved, and bought tons of sharpies and sandpaper and anything else we could think of.

She and I spent most of our weekends in her room, Scott usually with us, roughing up her furniture and writing sayings and drawing pictures on them. I was pretty sure there was a dick on the back of her nightstand, but I never mentioned it out loud, just shot Scott a look. He'd grinned at me, and I'd almost forgotten why I was annoyed.

Almost.

Matt made Prom King that year for about four seconds while he said a thank you to the school and then passed off his crown to the nearest guy available so he wouldn't have to dance with Claire Yates. The school hadn't approved, but whatever Matt had said to the principal about it had evidently made it clear it wasn't a fight he wanted to have.

Claire's popularity downsized from it. She never really forgave him, either.

Once I started really trusting Dr. Hoar, digging into my issues was a hell of a lot easier. I could see how much she was helping me. I even knew that I felt better. One day I pointed out a fucking sunset to Scott, amazed by the colors in the sky, and he couldn't stop smiling at me for three solid hours.

As time moved on and more and more space was put between me and my suicide attempt, I felt my personality reshaping. Gone was the kid who didn't like the outdoors, who hated being around people, who couldn't handle the idea of being alive. I was still me, deep down, still sarcastic and introverted and wary of people, but I was *more* too. I had dreams, and hobbies, and I smiled more easily and enjoyed things more fully.

I dropped my therapy sessions from twice a week to once, then twice a month, then whenever I needed them. I was a lighter, happier person, and I owed it all to the people around me who refused to give up on me. I started saying "I love you" without fear, without the connotation that it would be the last thing anyone heard from me. I laughed, and joked. I *lived*.

Scott hit a hard place somewhere near the end of his Junior year. He ended up in the hospital after hurting himself while drunk out of his mind. I guessed it was the kind of wake up call his mother needed though, because it made her get her shit together. His parents divorced, and she showed up at our house asking Scott to go back home with her. He told her he needed time to think about it.

Juliet somehow made it through her entire Junior year, hanging out with Scott, Matt, Kaitlynn and myself, but it obviously wasn't enough and Bridgewood Academy was taking its toll on her. Eventually, we had a family meeting about moving.

Grant wasn't far, but it would put space between me and school, and Uncle Ben and work. There was a house for sale between Grant and Bridgewood that he'd always liked, and he didn't mind the back and forth. It'd seemed to me that Juliet should be the one to commute, since she was the only one making any real changes, but he'd looked at me and simply said there were things in this house that were ready to be left behind.

It was the house Aunt Lily had died in, it was the house I'd moved into after trying to kill myself, it was the studio that still smelled like pot and the bedroom from his childhood that Rick never could seem to escape. As a family, we'd agreed. Grant it was.

I also didn't mind putting space between my parents and myself either. I hadn't accidentally run into them anywhere, but it was bound to happen one day, and I liked the lowered statistics of a new town.

Scott decided not to go with us, and to move back in with his mom instead. It was a decision that took a lot of work, but in the end, he and his mom had been working hard on their relationship, and it felt right to him. It was hard to leave him behind, but the separation was temporary. Most of his stuff stayed with me, and so did he, most nights out of the week.

That summer we packed our things and made the move. Rick left us to get an apartment downtown, but we all had a feeling he'd be around quite a lot regardless, and Juliet seemed to breathe easier the day Grant High accepted her transcripts. She was healthy, these days. But while I had learned to be less guarded, Juliet had somehow learned to be more. I didn't necessarily think it was a bad thing, but it made me worry about her.

Sober Juliet was a lot more fun than her counterpart though, and she learned to indulge without hurting herself. No more drugs, but a drink on occasion. Just one, at least until she was legal. We went out sometimes, just to dance, just to feel looser. I found us a nice gay club in the city. It kind of became our spot for the summer.

Healing took time, but we managed.

And living was definitely worth it.

***

It was raining outside, hard enough I could hear it beating against the roof, the occasional splash of thunder and lightning. It rained a lot more in Grant than it ever did in Bridgewood.

"Are those college applications already?"

Scott fell over my shoulders behind me, his chin dropping onto my head. I splayed my hand over the paperwork. "Don't let it scare you."

"School just started," he said, his voice gone thin. I hadn't figured out just what about it bothered him so much. The unknown, the future, the possibility of separation? As if I would go anywhere without him.

In fact, that was kind of the point. Technically, I was just a Junior, but if I managed to stay on the fast track I'd graduate with him. Which meant I needed my college shit figured out as soon as possible. I reached up and grabbed his arms, tugging until he slid around enough that I could kiss him. "I'm just getting a head start, the way I always do, stop panicking."

"M'not panicking," he muttered against my lips, and I smiled before he kissed me again. "You want more hot chocolate?"

Homemade hot chocolate had become our newest addiction, and I nodded greedily. Scott kissed my cheek and picked up my empty mug before going to the kitchen.

I turned my attention back to the application question that had been causing me trouble: *"If you could sum up the last few years of your life in two words, what would they be?"* I hated lifestyle questions. I never felt creative enough to answer them. This one was mocking me, because it was all I had left before I could submit it. It'd been two whole days.

I heard the front door open, signaling Juliet's arrival. Bridgewood Academy had closed for the day because of the weather, but Grant only let out early. There were two distinct pairs of footsteps. She was with someone.

Scott was asking who her friend was, and I could picture his curious smile clearly.

"This is Lena," Juliet said, and she pronounced it *Len-ah*. "Lena, this is Scott. He lives here most of the time."

I heard the new girl ask Scott about football and decided they'd lost my interest. I focused on my applications again until I realized Scott had never brought me my damn hot chocolate.

"Baby!" I whined out, and gave him a few minutes to answer before I called for him again. I could hear him talking, which meant the bastard was ignoring me.

My stomach growled.

I sighed and climbed to my feet, stretching out before heading to the hallway.

"Baaaabyyy," I tried again, arms crossed, waiting to be paid attention to. Scott caught my eye and looked annoyed, but I knew he loved me. "I'm hungry."

He turned toward the kitchen with an eye-roll and I sent the newcomer a quick look. She was cute, brunette hair down in damp waves, jade green eyes, all wrapped up in a soft-looking sweater. I knew Scott was going to hate me but I couldn't resist the need to test her. "Baby!"

He dropped his head back dramatically on his shoulders. "*What, Lakyn?*"

"Love me!" Did I stomp my foot? Theatric. I threw on a pout for the hell of it and had to fight my smile off as Scott twisted around, the corners of his mouth lifting. He crossed the space between us, cupped my face in his hands, and leaned in for a kiss. It was a good one, too. Soft and gentle and personal. I waited until I heard footsteps on the stairs before I let him pull away.

Juliet and her new friend were headed up to her bedroom, and I grinned at Scott. "Thank you."

"Little shit," he criticized.

I shrugged, unbothered. "You love it."

"True," he allowed. "I was feeling her out just fine on my own, you know."

"Sure." I patted his arm and led the way into the kitchen, picking up my forgotten mug from earlier and refilling it. "What do you want for supper?"

"You're the hungry one," he pointed out.

I hummed at that. "Cooking channel?"

He nodded and we surfed through a few options, keeping the volume down so we could listen for the signs of a fight upstairs. I was sure Juliet knew what we were doing, and could picture her disapproving glare, but I didn't care. We had her best interests in mind.

"I like her so far," Scott said. "Lena, I mean."

"You like everyone."

"And you hate everyone. It's why we make a good team. Balance."

I smirked and abandoned my mission to wrap my arms around his neck and pull him in for a kiss. He went easily, his hands slipping down my back and under my pajama bottoms. My hips jerked from skin-on-skin contact, and I laughed against his mouth.

We let ourselves indulge for a moment then pulled apart to focus on finding something to eat. Enchiladas seemed like a good idea, and we washed our hands and shared one more kiss before Scott called, "Juliet! Come help with dinner! Bring your hot friend!"

I glared at him, he laughed.

When the girls came downstairs Juliet looked more relaxed, but still guarded, and a glance at Lena said we somehow hadn't run her off with our gayness yet. I still hadn't decided how I felt, but she was earning points.

"I can't cook," she said, wide-eyed and worried. "I mean, I can't even handle a grilled cheese levels of can't cook."

"You don't actually have to help," Juliet said, but Scott laughed and followed her with, "I'm sure we can find something for you."

He put Lena in charge of cutting the chicken, and then we went about our business as usual. She didn't stick out, like I expected her to. In fact, she worked around us rather well. She answered Scott's endless questions without being annoyed, and grinned at Juliet anytime they looked at each other. I spent more time watching her than I did actually doing my job, and when she brought me the finished chicken I managed to smile at her.

She beamed like she'd won a cookie or something.

Somehow we managed to actually get everything ready. Chicken and cheese enchiladas, beans, rice, sopapillas for dessert. I felt pride swell up inside of me, the way it always seemed to after finishing a meal. Even though it was less needed as a coping mechanism these days, it was a reminder that I didn't hurt anymore.

"You know, for a house full of white kids, this doesn't look half bad," Lena praised. Juliet chuckled. Oh, another point.

Scott shot her one of his stupidly bright smiles. "See, I told you it would be okay if you helped! Nothing burned! Not even the house!"

Lena elbowed him and he turned his smile on me. Like he was trying to say, *See! We can like her!*

I rolled my eyes as I heard the front door open, meaning my uncle and Rick were home. Juliet ran off to greet them, but it didn't take long before they were all back. Uncle Ben pulled me into a headlock and I cursed and struggled but no one bothered to help. Rude assholes.

"Who's this?" he asked, meaning Lena.

"New girl, Jules?" Rick put in, and even without being able to see, I knew tension had risen in the room. I wasn't sure if the question was a test of Rick's own or if he was just dumb, but I figured the latter.

My uncle released me and I went for Scott's hand without thinking. Juliet was obviously bothered but Lena just looked confused. I watched as the realization dawned on her that Rick had been asking if she was Jules' new girlfriend. It would be funny, if it wasn't such a moment. Juliet punched her brother in the shoulder and he leaned away from her with a wounded expression.

"Lena's just a friend, Rick," she stressed between clenched teeth. "Can we eat?"

Uncle Ben shot Rick a look and I wondered briefly if my family had always been this *'movie made for TV'* dramatic or if this was a new development. Rick recovered by praising the dinner spread.

"Scott, Lena is it?" my uncle asked, and when she nodded he motioned toward the kitchen. "Come here for a minute."

I had a feeling it was probably about the weather and let go of Scott so he could go talk. His mother didn't always like how much time he spent at our place. I had a feeling it was a sex thing, but I didn't bother to get into it.

The second they were gone, Juliet rounded on her brother. "Just because I bring a girl home doesn't immediately mean —"

"I'm sorry," Rick said. "It's just that you usually don't…"

I knew 'have friends' was on the tip of his tongue so I gave a jerk of my head and Rick lifted his hands in surrender. "You're getting awfully defensive about your not-girlfriend."

"Rick, I swear to god, if you run her off —"

"Stop!" I interrupted. "We can fight later. There's food."

Juliet glared at him once more before taking her usual spot, and after a moment he followed her lead. I understood where Rick was coming from, it'd been a good year or so since she'd bothered to bring anyone home, but I doubted making a scene was the way to keep it happening.

Apparently, my uncle agreed with my way of thinking, because he took his own seat before asking how everyone's day was. None of us touched our food until Lena and Scott returned, and Rick sighed gratefully.

"Finally! Who's saying grace?"

Lena took the seat next to me with the kind of familiar comfort that made it seem like that had always been her spot. She looked a little uncomfortable at the idea of saying grace, but she took my hand anyway. Another point, I supposed.

It was Scott's turn for the prayer. He wasn't very religious these days, and I was always surprised when he actually did it. "Father God: thank you for this food, please bless it to our bodies, we ask in Jesus' name. Thank you for this family, which has been so good to each other and to me. Thank you for Lakyn, and how much he loves me. Still, somehow. Lord, I know you know he puts up with a lot."

I had a theory that when Scott said grace he wasn't really speaking to God but to us. He liked to say his thanks in a way that wasn't repetitive or overbearing. Where no one had to say anything back. It was that thought that made me squeeze Lena's hand without meaning to.

"Thank you for Lena, because everyone knows Juliet could use a friend." I opened my eyes to slant a look toward him and saw Juliet move in a way I was sure was to kick him. "And thank you for the rain. So that we get to stay here. All. Night. Long."

Sometimes I really hated that Scott thought he was funny. He cleared his throat and finished with, "Amen."

We copied him and then it was free game on the food. Scott and I had a system perfected to grab each other's favorites if it was in reaching distance, so I was stacking three sopapillas on his plate when I heard Rick ask, "Why do we allow this kid to say grace?"

"Because he's family," Uncle Ben answered without hesitation, and I ignored the way my chest still got tight over words like that. Scott smiled and pressed a soft kiss to the side of my neck. I pretended like it didn't mean as much to me as it did.

I didn't stop watching Lena, even after we all had our food and conversation struck up around us. She managed to keep up, even with jokes she didn't fully get and half told stories between laughter. Scott and Juliet were both good at filling in the blanks for her. She didn't have the air of someone who was socially comfortable anywhere, but she seemed okay here. She wasn't tensing up over all the gay, anyway. It was a little annoying, I was going out of my way to push her down, but she was holding her ground. On the other hand, that was good news for Jules.

Dinner was an affair like it usually was, filled with jokes and laughs and vibrant retelling of our days. Long gone were the times when we all ate alone, or in complete silence. No one in this family was tired anymore. No one was hurting.

Lena jumped up to help clean when we finished and I shook my head before placing a hand on her wrist. "Don't worry about it."

"We have a system," Rick explained from across the table, already picking up plates. "Half of us does the cooking, the other half does the cleaning."

My uncle nodded to back him. "You kids go off and have fun. Scott, Lakyn, behave."

I had a feeling that had more to do with us not eavesdropping on the girls than anything we might actually get up to, but I stuck my tongue out at him anyway.

Scott's arms went around me and he dragged me off upstairs.

"I like her," he said again, kicking the bedroom door shut and falling down on our bed. "I think she'll be good for Jules."

I hummed noncommittally and got the Xbox out, throwing a controller on his chest.

"Hey," he said, wrapping a hand around my arm and pulling me down for a quick kiss. "I love you."

"Yeah," I muttered. "I love me, too."

Scott snorted and pushed me away. "You are such a little shit."

I cracked up laughing and fell down next to him, starting up the game. But as the words bounced around in my head, I realized that it was true. I did love myself; it'd taken me a long time to get there, but it'd happened. Part of me had a feeling it'd taken a long time for a lot of people to love me.

"If you could sum up the last few years of your life in two words, what would they be?"

I smiled. I had the answer to the question.

Loving Lakyn.

LOVING LAKYN

The *Something Just Like Love* Series

Loving Lakyn
Just Juliet
Saving Scott *(Coming Soon)*
Losing Lena *(Coming Soon)*

Charlotte Reagan

Printed in Great Britain
by Amazon